Beyond the Marry-Go-Round

a novel by

Herb Dimock

EDDY PUBLISHING

ISBN: 0-9722835-1-X

Second Printing—2005

Request for information should be addressed to:

Eddy Publishing
PO BOX 1084
Carnation WA 98104-1084
425 333-6915
E-mail: dimock4@centurytel.net

Cover Design: Michelle S. Lenkner – SterlingHouse Publisher
Book Design: Teri Paulus of Design Works

Printed in the United States of America

Dedicated to

Gilbert Mathew

• Confidant •

• Critic •

• Collaborator •

Contents

1 White Cloud

August heat drove Sally perilously close to the brink of inner collapse, which she had been fighting for six months. She and Mike were not talking. She had tried week after week to get her mate to work at planning the next steps for the family's economic life but was met only with deepening silence. *This will pass,* she argued with herself*, the way California heat always passes.* But she saw at last that the children were beginning to reflect signs of anxiety as faithful mirrors of their parents.

On Saturday morning, Sally stared out their front window as two sets of neighbors in bathing suits loaded up their cars to escape the soaring Grass Valley temperatures. *The pool at Memorial Park?* she thought. *Or maybe the river?* The images of cool water that splashed through her mind, cried hauntingly, urging escape.

She turned back and found Mike standing in the kitchen doorway, hands on his hips, staring at her. "Air conditioner's dead," he grumbled. "Couldn't fix it. Gotta get out of here."

Sally kept her rising eagerness on a tight leash. "All right." A vision of swimming in the river called to her with cooling promise. They could escape.

And then Mike surprised her with a mumbled message that, she felt, seemed off-handed. "Gotta talk."

He wants to talk? Sally was almost afraid to believe what she was hearing. She kept her silence as she had a hundred times in the past month, and while Mike went out to get their Toyota in readiness, she hustled to fill a lunch basket and scramble together their swim suits. *He wants to talk? About what? Will he hear me? Is he ready to let go of his stupid silence?*

Mike's chore of strapping 4-year-old Jeannie into the back seat was an ordeal which Sally always watched with uneasiness. Mike insisted on doing it his own way, roughly, against her protests. Six-year-old Tad accomplished his own seating with sturdy independence.

Mike avoided eye-contact with her as they settled into their front-seat posts. He backed out onto Lidster Avenue, and Sally picked up the challenge, deliberately matching his grumbling tone with choppy protests.

"All right. Where are we going?" She was urgent.

"White Cloud."

"I thought you'd go to the river." Was she going to be forced into a fight for what the family needed?

"Everybody'll be there."

"Bridgeport isn't the only spot."

"Do you want us to be alone, or not?" he snapped.

"The children need to go swimming."

Mike ignored her and headed for Highway 20.

"Where we goin', Mama?" cried Tad from the back seat.

"Your father has decided that we have to go to the ridge," Sally replied in a sour tone. "To White Cloud."

"It'll be cooler. And empty," Mike added with finality. "Now be quiet."

"You said we could go swimming," Jeannie whined, but Mike was silent.

Sally's gloom sank deeper. Was there no way out of their nightmarish world?

They left Grass Valley behind, slipped quickly past neighboring Nevada City and steered for the high country of the Sierra Nevada foothills.

Sally began again. "Every time I try to talk you run away."

"Can't you wait till we get where we're going?"

"It's always the same. Tomorrow, tomorrow."

"We are going to talk," Mike spoke sharply. "I agree with you. We've stalled too long. Now give me a break."

Sally stared out the open window, the heated air beating against her face. The Toyota's air conditioning, also, had long since broken down, and there was no money for repairs. No money for anything any more. No way to escape the trap of Mike's job loss, and her failure to fill the gap adequately with seamstress' income.

The trip along Washington Ridge past Five Mile House dragged her into deeper pain. The spindly second-growth pines rising on either side of the highway transformed it into a canyon. A breeze rustled the dark branches and Sally thought it whispered, "There's no way...no way...out."

She closed her eyes and breathed in the smell of hot pines. Mike was always complaining about the Gold Rush days, when cut-and-slash logging stripped the ridge of its native forest. The scraggly trees through which they were traveling were a bitter reminder of what had started their present trouble. Mike had dared to blow the whistle when the Forest Service allowed a lumber company to illegally clear-cut 50 acres, then 60 acres, then 80 along the Yuba River. She had battled against his growing determination to squeal, and her warnings proved true. He lost his job. That's when their suffering shifted into the open. Their buried disagreements became heated combat.

What has gone wrong with the family spirit? Usually, he has been in control; now he always seems driven. For two years his only work has been part-time at a hamburger stand. He's always depressed. Fights back against my suggestions. No wonder the kids are cranky every day.

Sally opened her eyes just before they zoomed past the 4000-foot elevation marker. "Do you have to drive so fast?" she complained. "This isn't the freeway."

Mike didn't answer. She felt his haste to reach the sign announcing the Forest Service picnic grounds was part of his feeling driven. She doubted that arriving would make any difference.

White Cloud had special meaning for Sally. Her thoughts flashed back to the beautiful Saturday in June seven years ago. It was the most romantic time of her young life. She and Mike took the day off to explore the high country. They parked in the picnic grounds and went jogging along the woodland path that traced the flat top of the ridge. It was wide and inviting and smooth. After a stretch they found a log to sit on, to let their panting breath slow down. That was when Mike wrapped his arms around her with their most passionate kiss ever. And then they moved to a hiding place behind the dense underbrush. That was when Tad was conceived. The beginning of trouble.

Tears crowded into Sally's eyelids as she recalled the day that changed the course of their lives. *What could they have done differently?* She had no answer.

There! There it is. White Cloud. Now what?

Mike slowed down, swerved left past a pair of elderly joggers, and Sally let go of a small bit of her anxiety as he drove deeper into the forested retreat.

"What did I tell you?" Mike muttered wearily. "It's empty. And it's cool. Okay?"

He switched off the engine near a pair of brown-painted picnic tables. While Sally unstrapped the children, he retrieved a pair of play shovels and buckets from the car trunk. *Thank God for the ponderosas,* she thought. Their wide-spread branches filtered the sunlight, protecting the carpet of pine needles beneath them and covering the tables in shadow. Sally watched Tad and Jeannie grab their toys and head for a sheltered spot a dozen paces down the path.

Impulsively she grabbed Mike's forearm. "It's not as cool as you think," she said with a frown. She intended affection with her touch, but he pulled loose from her grip. He drifted away to one of the picnic tables and sat on the top, resting his feet on the bench.

Sally rummaged in the back seat of the car and dragged out a cushion, the one she always needed when driving. She set it down on a spot more than two feet away from her husband and joined him in watching the children as they dug tunnels and built castles in the soft earth. At last, Sally broke their standoff.

"We need to make a new start, Mike."

"It won't work," he snapped with a quick glance.

"Don't be so negative." She felt her fears deepen. "Why can't you talk about the good stuff?"

"Like what?" His challenge was harsh and cynical. His eyes seemed full of black anger.

"We paid off the Toyota."

"Big deal."

"My seamstress business gets more profitable every month." *Profitable?* she thought to herself, *but our debt only gets deeper and deeper.* "And what's more I've got a helper working for me now," she boasted.

Mike spit out his words. "Sure. Best possible way to remind me that I don't make enough to support the family. Every day!"

"You're too sensitive."

"You're too bitchy. There's nothing you can't find to complain about." His words were muffled, and Sally was sure he was trying to keep the children from hearing.

She nudged back at him as softly as she could. "Who's being bitchy now?"

"Well, I don't have to stand it any more."

Sally looked at him in surprise. "What are you talking about?" she asked with tense curiosity.

He fiddled with a loose pine needle that had fallen on the table-top. "I got the job in Eureka," he muttered.

"You what?" Sally asked, half in unbelief.

"Yeah. Phone call came yesterday."

With bursting exuberance and rising spirits, she pressed on. "Mike! You mean you're the new manager of Northwest Lumber?"

"Not that job." He almost laughed. "Only a part-time supervisor."

"But isn't this our breakthrough?" She groped for some kind of solid ground to stand on.

"No way. It doesn't pay that much. And I really hate working for people who could be cutting old growth. But at least I can watch from the inside."

Sally swallowed hard. This was not the breakthrough after all. "It would mean we'd have to move, wouldn't it? We wouldn't be any farther ahead than we are now. You're not going to accept, are you?"

She threw her question at him, and for what seemed like an eternity the silence grew heavier between them, until at last Mike, half talking to himself, mumbled, "It's time for us to split."

His message didn't come clear. Sally pushed against the oppressive silence with growing fear in her heart. "What are you talking about?"

Mike sat up straighter and his words were hard. "There's no point in kidding ourselves that we can live together any longer. I'm filing for divorce."

Sally began to fight back with words of denial, then paused. For months Mike's trend had been unclear. She had felt herself torn between her need to provide for the children and her commitment to their marriage. Now she didn't know what to feel or say.

Suddenly, she saw Tad throw a handful of dirt into his sister's face. Jeannie screamed. Sally bolted from her seat and ran to the play area.

"You do that again, Tad, and I'll give you the worst spanking you ever dreamed of." Her anger was rising. The impossible chaos of having to cope with a broken family was more than she could handle. She knelt by her daughter to wipe away the dirt. "Jeannie, Jeannie. Hang your head down and let the tears wash out the sand." She worked with a handkerchief until most of the grit was gone.

Sally was afraid to return to her seat on the top of the picnic table. She had no clue how to deal with Mike's shocker. She lingered at the play area, stunned by the thought of a divorce and her family's destruction.

That can't be. How could we support two households three hundred miles apart? Expenses would be much greater. I'd have to find full-time work, and baby sitters. We might even lose the house. Her ocean of tears, now driven by storm, was almost beyond control. Finally, she rose to her feet with a painful sigh to return to the table.

What she saw disturbed her deeply. Ten feet behind their seating was another couple, sitting quietly on a picnic table, just as she and Mike had sat minutes earlier.

The pair appeared to be older. Both had white hair and were dressed in shorts and tee shirts. Could these be the people she had seen jogging near the entrance?

They smiled and, as Sally came back to where Mike was

sitting, the man spoke in a friendly fashion.

"Children have a lot to learn about getting along with each other."

The sound of another voice stirred Mike, and he turned quickly to check the source.

"Children need the firm discipline that only a family can provide," the woman said in a kind voice.

Sally stopped by the end of their picnic table, speechless. Mike joined her. Was he offering of some kind of support? The image of the white-haired people sitting together seemed strangely enlarged to her, not threatening, but awesome somehow. They roused a buried memory from her childhood of how she had felt about her grandparents when they came to visit; so large and important and different from her Mom and Dad.

When the couple slipped off their table and took steps closer, Sally realized that they were both normal in height after all.

The man spoke with a touch of humor. "It can shake a person to find out that he is not alone. Some of the best things in life come when people get together."

Instinctively Sally pressed closer to Mike. Never had she felt so divided about meeting new people. She wanted to flee back to the privacy of the highway, but at the same time she felt peculiarly attracted to the couple.

And then Sally felt small hands clutching her bare legs. It was Tad and Jeannie drawn from their play by the sound of unfamiliar voices.

"Well," said the man, waving a hand toward the children and filling the awkward silence with the sound of good cheer, "this hardly looks like a broken family, does it? Everybody's snuggling together."

"What do you mean, 'broken'?" Sally said defensively. Had the old guy overheard her and Mike's private words?

"Yes, Sally, didn't we hear Mike tell you that he was going to file for divorce?" The man spoke quietly.

The shock of her name used by complete strangers prompted Sally to press herself even closer against Mike. She took courage that he also was edging toward her, a momentary signal of unity.

The old man knelt down to the children's level and, with a warm smile, held out his arms in welcome. *What in the world is he doing?* Sally reached out to grip her daughter's shoulder to keep her from responding, but she was too late. Jeannie ran into the man's arms, and Tad followed a second later.

Sally watched her children's delight in their new friends. A wave of guilt broke over her. For weeks she had been so distracted by Mike's moodiness that she spent very little time cuddling with the kids.

The man was the ultimate grandpa, firm and kind and radiant with lightheartedness. There was something magnetic about his eyes and his smile. Curiously, however, his powerfully mature face was free of wrinkles and age spots. He poked fun with Tad and Jeannie, triggering their laughter, which she had not heard for months. Sally smiled in spite of herself.

"Tad...Jeannie," he said gently, "aren't you glad your parents are ready for a new beginning?"

Sally felt a tremor pass through Mike. This was clearly not the direction he intended to follow at all.

"When we watched your car turn into the campground," the woman added, nodding at Sally and at Mike, "we saw a black cloud surrounding your car. You looked as though you needed help."

"What are you talking about?" Sally protested. "There was no black cloud!" A flood of shame was rising within. If she and Mike couldn't solve their problems they had no business staying together. It was her worst horror. She looked to him for support, but his words shocked her.

"Yeah. That's right. Got a black cloud, for sure."

No, no, no! Sally's protest exploded within. Already pounded by his decision to pursue divorce, she was now being battered by his sharing the truth with people who were totally foreign to them.

"So, who are you anyway?" The demand leaped out. "Why should you care about our private affairs?"

The woman spoke softly. "Forgive us for not introducing ourselves. Please call me Sophie, and he is Josh." She laid a gentle hand on her man's head while he still was kneeling with the children.

"Okay." Mike spoke with a wistful softness. "So it's Josh and Sophie. How could you see a black cloud over us?"

"Yes, it's hanging over you right now," Josh answered. "Aren't you imagining that a broken family will be better than what you have now."

Mike answered virtuously, "Well, why not?"

"Ah! There it is! Isn't this what everybody's doing? The culture of America says it's all right! That's what you are clinging to, isn't it, Mike? The American culture. But what makes you think it will work? Divorce will be worse for all of you."

Silently Sally cheered, but her fear grew. She was not satisfied simply to hear the names of these people. Where did they come from? Why could they speak so strongly? Yet something about this woman, Sophie, began to reach out to her with healing touch. She was beautiful. Her wonderful crown of white hair and the light in her face projected a peaceful mood. Her spirit of intimacy was powerful.

Finally Sally stammered, "Yes, I — guess — we do have a black cloud." And as her confession came out into the open she also felt a growing uneasiness about loading all their pain onto Tad and Jeannie.

"Come on, kids. Let's get back to your sand castle."

Sophie spoke gently. "Don't you think it might be very helpful for the children to share in working through this family problem?"

Their eyes lit up with eagerness and both Tad and Jeannie nodded vigorously. Sally had to agree. There was important truth in what the lady was saying.

Josh picked up on the picture of the cloud his mate had proposed. "So how long has it been shadowing you?"

"For at least two years." Sally found herself torn between her desire for privacy and a haunting pull in the depths of her soul crying for help.

"What happened two years ago?" Sophie asked.

Sally groped for a clearer picture. "It's just that every time I try to talk to Mike, he walks away."

"I'll tell you what happened," Mike thrust in with his old passion. "Two years ago I lost my job with the Forest Service."

"How come?" said Josh.

"I leaked secrets to the public."

"About?"

"They were allowing clear-cutting that would be totally destructive."

"Good for you!" said Sophie. "But, Mike, how did that lead to your black cloud?"

"That's when Sal began to climb on my back. Always pushing. Every day! I guess I got fed up," he ended lamely.

Sally glanced quickly at Mike. His anger was clearly losing ground now, and she could see that he knew it.

Sophie added more wisdom. "We are very sure, Mike, that you have been wounded. Not only by the Forest Service. Search your childhood also. How did your parents scar you?"

He was visibly disturbed, shifting his body awkwardly. Finally he nodded and spoke almost to himself. "Yeah. Too true. I don't like to think about it."

From his crouching position with the children Josh spoke up. "It's not surprising that you imagine divorce is the way out."

Tad, still close under a grandfatherly arm with a worried expression spreading across his face, reached for understanding. "What's divorce?"

Sally squirmed. Was it wrong that she had not talked to her children about the "Great American Cop-out"?

Josh rose to his feet and focused a challenging gaze on Tad's two parents. "Do you want to explain to your children? Or shall I?"

A moment of awkward silence followed. Sally glanced uneasily at Mike. Finally he moved to the picnic table, sat on the bench and held out his arms to invite the children to come to him.

"Divorce," he began, groping for the right words. "Divorce is when a mother and a father can't live in the same house together."

Tad struggled to make the connection. "Who's going away?"

Mike fell silent again, still searching for words, and the moment was broken when Josh stepped closer to the father and son and offered an answer for both of them.

"Tad, one thing is for sure. Families are forever— even broken families. Your mom and dad will always be your parents."

Sophie joined them. "Marriages can be ended, but not families." She turned directly to Mike. "Don't you need to think a bit more carefully today? You have another choice. You don't have to create a broken family. You have the option of a time of separation." She stepped closer to him. "Mike, wouldn't it be possible for you to go to your new job in Eureka and let the healing process take over? Think about it."

Is there anything they don't know about us? Sally whispered to herself. For the first time a cool wave of comfort seeped into her consciousness. How could these people touch the core of their lives so quickly and so gently? As she watched in silence the awesomeness of their encounter struck deeper. Separation? Not divorce? Josh and Sophie were not run-of-the-mill Americans. They projected an aura of a new kind of world. She felt her heartbeat grow stronger. She stole a glance at her husband. What really is going through his consciousness? She held her breath.

Mike's gaze shifted back and forth between Tad and Jeannie. "I don't know if it would make any difference, just to be separated. I was feeling a break would be the better way. What would we do 300 miles apart?"

"The first thing that could happen," Sophie responded, "is that the level of daily irritations would shrink to almost zero. That would give time for other things to come into focus."

Josh thrust into the exchange with a voice of gentle authority. "One of the great principles that many young people miss is this, that the purpose of marriage is to create family. Marriage is not first about feeling happy. That can happen only after Mike and Sally learn to put the family first. And 'family' for you two, now, means Tad and Jeannie. That's the place of beginning."

Sally wanted to clap her hands in joyful agreement, but her inner voice held firm in watchful waiting.

Josh extended the picture. "At this moment of choice in your life, Mike, you cannot see ahead to the tragedy a divorce would load onto your children. They are the ones who would be wounded most severely. The scars would go deep. The same way you were wounded when your parents divorced."

Josh reached across the open space to lay a hand on Tad's shoulder in a gesture of solidarity and encouragement. He looked squarely into Mike's eyes. "We urge you to use this opportunity at Eureka to create a breathing space for all of you. A separation that could lead to a chance to start over."

Yes, yes, yes, thought Sally. *He needs to start over.* She was about to turn to Mike to help increase the pressure on his soul, when Sophie added more to their message.

"And, Sally, this can be a time for you to give healing a chance to reach the broken parts of your soul."

Sally's awe began to spread into long neglected corners of her consciousness. A momentary image flashed: the time when her father whipped her for a sassy refusal to pick up the rubbish in her room; and how she secretly left messes under her bed from that time on.

These people standing before her were powerful and full of light beyond anything she had ever imagined before. As the sun moved toward the zenith it sent warm rays directly toward Mike. She watched him look up with longing as the white heads of Josh and Sophie hovered over him. They clearly were bestowing a new coolness of spirit for he breathed in a deep sigh of ease.

Sally searched from face to face groping for guidance, and then Mike stood up. He looked into her eyes.

"Our friends here have helped me see that we do have

other options. I think maybe it will be good for the family if I go to Eureka for a while."

"Do you mean you're going ahead with divorce?" Sally spoke the negative, praying for the better answer.

"No. I think that's on the shelf for now." Mike struggled on. Was a new reality embracing him? He spoke softly, once again as though to himself. "This is just a temporary separation,"

"But how can we be a family three hundred miles apart?" Sally was still far from being convinced.

Mike shrugged his shoulders. "You should keep the Toyota. You and the kids can visit from time to time. And if I get any time off I can take the bus home."

Jeannie, catching something of the hopefulness of the moment, clambered up onto the bench to stand by her father's side, as though to join the new level of feeling. Tad followed, to hold on to his father's arm.

Sally did not miss the beautiful message the children were giving. *They are understanding more than either of us imagined,* she thought. But for her the prospect of "separation" was still a shadow that loomed with its threat of divorce. She didn't have confidence that she could handle the harsh prospect.

Nevertheless, for her the cloud of darkness had been replaced by a white cloud, and that did let in fresh light. She turned to their new mentors with gratitude.

"I want to thank you for taking time with us. Are you professional marriage counselors?"

"We help wherever we can," said Sophie without giving direct answer. "We are eager to encourage a new vision of marriage for America."

"That's great," Sally murmured, and as the reality of the noontime hour pressed in upon her, she added, "Will you be willing to have lunch with us? I'm sure we have enough to share."

"Thank you for the offer," Josh responded. "But, no, we should be on our way."

Without another word he and Sophie linked hands and turned to resume their jogging. For Sally it felt as though joy was running away. She held on to Tad and Jeannie who were ready to run with them. She saw that the action of Josh and Sophie was disturbing for Mike. He was not about to let the contact with these wonderful people slip away. He took several steps after the departing couple and called out with urgency.

"Please, is there some way we could get in touch with you?"

They paused in their jogging and turned toward him.

"I mean," he pressed forward in fumbling confession, "I mean, there may come a time when we'll need more help."

"Of course," said Sophie. She nudged Josh, and he pulled out of the pocket of his shorts a calling card.

"This is our cell phone number," said Josh. He patted the tiny black unit hooked onto his belt. "You can touch base with us at any time." He passed the card into Mike's hand and then smiled at Sophie. Without further words they started again on their trip.

Sally found her body reacting as though she were going to follow them wherever they might go on their jogging journey. Mike returned to stand beside her. Together they watched until the white heads disappeared among the trees.

In her heart of hearts Sally felt that the tug of war between herself and Mike was still alive. The shifting gravel underfoot gave her no assurance. Maybe they had been granted a recess. Maybe they could find a way to rescue the family. Maybe not.

She turned to stare into her husband's eyes, searching for more firm ground on which to stand. "Are you really willing to postpone divorce?"

He responded meditatively. "I think I should make my trip to Eureka tomorrow." She watched him fumble with the calling card and its number. He turned it over to the back side. And then he shook his head in puzzlement.

"Look, Sal." He passed the card to her. "Maybe this really is our task."

The bold print leaped off the page.

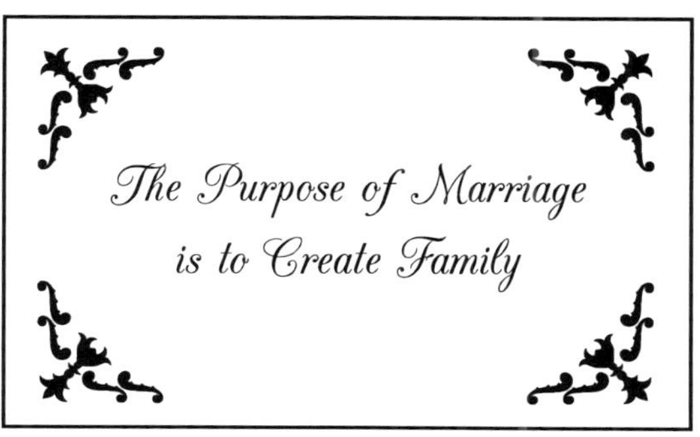

The Purpose of Marriage is to Create Family

Eureka

A month of busy days at the Lidster Avenue house pushed Sally and the children at last toward the Labor Day weekend. This was to be their first opportunity to make the promised trip to visit Daddy at his new home and job. For Tad and Jeannie it would be an exciting new adventure and a time to tell their father about school that had just begun. But for Sally the impending contact with Mike sharpened her anxiety.

Three phone calls that she made during the month had been much too brief. After sharing a couple of minutes of basic information about his boarding house and job and financial problems, he had apologized, “Sorry, Sal, I’ve got to go. We can talk more next time.” But each “next time” it was the same and deprived her of a chance to connect with the inner direction of his new life. She began to feel she was talking to a stranger.

Two days before the coming holiday she called her mother in Oakland in search of support. She wanted to talk out her feelings about the shadowing threat of divorce, but when the moment came she held back. She only told about the stresses of separation.

“He had to take the job, Mom. Otherwise we’d never catch up on mortgage payments.”

Mother focused on the children. “How are Tad and Jeannie getting along without their father?”

“It’s tough on them. They’re harder to manage. They miss him.” Sally wished she could avoid talking about the children’s behavior, but they were at the heart of the family’s problem.

“Do you miss Mike?” Mother pursued.

That was the penetrating question, and Sally’s answer came slowly. “I don’t know, Mom.”

After she hung up and sat quietly in a moment of

meditation a different answer pressed forward. I do miss him. But then there were the unanswered questions. Is his job going to hold him? Is he finding peace? Is there maybe another woman he has found? Is he still thinking divorce?

Before she could feel free to make the Eureka trip there was the dressmaking work to be taken care of. Karen, her treasured seamstress helper, needed to start on the new project that was promised for the following Wednesday. With patterns and cloth and accessories assembled in the back seat of the car, while the children were in school, Sally started out for Karen's humble home on Slate Creek Road. As always when she needed the skills of her sewing-machine-pro she felt the narrow limits of her own specialty, which was designing. She had a closet full of dress patterns she had developed but still no way to get them into the marketplace. Sally did function well as an employer and shared fairly the modest income from her bids on dress work.

As she pulled up to the curb she was glad again that her family didn't have to live in a cramped cottage like Karen's. It was another of the "low-cost" developments that the county had approved for poverty people; one of the Habitat for Humanity projects. Her own home on Lidster was very adequate.

"Hi, Sal," was Karen's standard greeting. "Come on in." She was younger than Sally by two or three years, a single mother with one toddler who was nicknamed Pinky because of her rosy cheeks. Karen's ragged clothing somehow didn't fit with her career as a sewing-machine specialist.

"I'm heading for Eureka tomorrow," said Sally, "and this job needs to be ready for Wednesday." She stood in the center of the crowded living room with her arms full of materials. "Do you think you can handle it?"

"Sure. Let's have a look." Her helper was always glad to work for extra income.

As Karen browsed over the patterns and instructions Sally felt a return of sadness over her friend's plight; one of the many single mothers she knew who were condemned to struggle alone for survival and the rearing of a child. To herself she muttered, *broken families are hell.*

"Any word from Joe?" Sally asked gently.

"Not a squeak. I think he's left town."

"How long's it been since he walked out?" Sally knew that Karen was much farther down the rough road than she herself.

"Six months," was the sour answer.

Pinky came stumbling closer to wrap arms around her mother's leg.

"Any new clues?" said Sally.

Karen looked up from the materials she held in her hands and curled her lips in a cynical smile. "Yeah. For sure. He found another girl." Sally could feel the buried bitterness.

She held back from sharing her own marriage problems, for her friend had enough to handle without taking on the burdens of another.

"So are you thinking divorce at last?"

"Have to."

Sally gave her a hug of encouragement. "Let me know if I can be helpful." She touched a loving hand on Pinky's head and headed back to Lidster Avenue.

Friday night laid on Sally one of the urgent times when she had to take both Tad and Jeannie into bed with her, one on each side, with only a sheet to cover them all during the warm dark hours. The coming trip had keyed them up with endless questions. "Is Eureka by the ocean?" "Can I sit in the front seat?" "Do we get to eat at MacDonalds?" "Can I take my dolls along?"...

Sally's patience and her skill with gentle rubbing of their heads finally led them into sleep. In the end she was the one who couldn't let go.

What's really going on with Mike? She talked to herself in the darkness with endless repetition. *He can still be thinking about divorce. —- It's an easy way out. — Even with those wonderful joggers urging him to try again, he can still forget. —- I wish I had that calling card with their number. — They surely could help with all the unknowns. — It wouldn't be smart for me to ask him for the number. — That would be pushing him.* — On and on she went with her doubts until exhaustion forced shut her restless eyelids.

She wanted to begin their journey at eight o'clock Saturday morning and had planned ahead creatively for the children's clothing: bathing suits if they had a chance to go swimming; warm garments if Eureka fog chose to dominate. She spent what seemed like fruitless time shaping her blond hair into attractive waves that wouldn't stay put. She dug out of the closet her own most glamorous dress, a simple silk with sequins around the collar. She prepared for sacks of lunch to be eaten along the way, and toys for play. Because she was such a meticulous planner, it was nine before the faithful Toyota was ready to roll down the Sierra slopes and cross the Sacramento Valley toward Highway 101, which would take them north.

The trip was hard, with children in the back seat snapping at each other, with Tad seeing signs of food as they sailed through Yuba City, clamoring for them to stop, with Jeannie regularly on the half hour whining that she had to "go pottie" when she didn't. Only after the middle of the afternoon when the children fell asleep from exhaustion did Sally have any free time to think.

The flood of anxiety about their coming encounter returned. Unwelcome thoughts again came washing into her mind. *The other-woman theme; am I headed down into the pit like Karen? Maybe that's why he's so abrupt over the phone. Doesn't he ever want to talk? Hiding in a cave. He's probably still wasting hours in front of the TV. Sleeping. Loafing. Lounging. Might as well be from another planet.*

They arrived in the Eureka environs after four-thirty. Sally pulled into a gas station to get directions about how to find Mike's place. She drove through twisted streets and finally located Mike waiting for them on the porch of his boarding house in the old part of town. As Sally brought the car to an abrupt stop both children snapped awake in time to see Daddy rise from his chair and start toward them. The instant their seat belts were released they ran toward the steps and into his outstretched arms. Sally followed and found herself as audience to a new drama.

Mike sat on the bottom step with a child on each knee and arms wrapped around them in loving embrace.

"I'm so happy to see you!" was his first word, and it was full of keen emotion that Sally had not heard before, warm and eager. His dark hair freshly cut was very smooth. Could this rough logger be the same man she had lived with back in Grass Valley? He poured his full attention onto the kids and left her standing alone, as though she were just a taxi driver.

"So, Jeannie, now you are in kindergarten. Tell me about it," was the beginning of his eager search.

"I'm in the first grade," Tad butted in with news of his world.

Jeannie struggled for an instant to keep her place-in-the-sun. "I draw with crayons," she protested and her eyes snapped at her brother.

Sally could see that Mike was hungering for their affection as he pressed on with his questioning.

"And, Tad, what have you found that's new in the first grade?"

"We're gonna learn to read books," he giggled.

"But didn't we teach you at home to read?"

"New books!" cried Tad. "Different books."

"Oh, I see. And Jeannie, what is your teacher's name?"

"Mrs. Danilovich."

"Wonderful," said Mike. He looked up at Sally finally and spoke positively. "I think we need to have some fun. There's a new circus in town."

"Shouldn't we visit your apartment first?" Sally protested.

"It's only one very small room." It was obvious he felt her suggestion was irrelevant.

"I mean shouldn't we take time to talk?"

"The kids have never seen a circus. There will be time tonight to talk—and tomorrow."

Sally's tension took a new turn. All of the piled up problems of their separation would have to wait: the strains of having to manage twin households, the uncertainties about their inner lives, the planning for future developments, all would have to wait. Her response was a reluctant, "Okay."

As they prepared to pile into the car Sally deferred to Mike. "Do you want to drive?" She was groping for ways to build bridges.

"No. You go ahead. I'll give directions."

He climbed into the back seat with a child under each arm and the baby-seats pushed aside. Sally started out again, and Mike gave her the cue.

"Take a left at the corner." His tone was jovial and she tried to relax.

Pressure from the core of her being pushed Sally to try for some way to launch a new beginning. She tossed a question over her shoulder. "Are you happy in your new job?"

"Not really. But it does bring in more money. Did you receive the check I sent last week?" She felt a touch of tension in his voice.

"It arrived on Monday. Without it I couldn't have made the trip. What's the matter with the job?"

"It's a dead-end. I'm beginning to think that any kind of logging is not good for Mother Earth."

"Daddy," Tad interrupted, "did you see my new sweat shirt with MacDonalds on the back?"

"Yes, I saw," said Mike, and Sally noted that he kept silent about his displeasure. She knew that he did not want his children to be agents of the advertising world.

"See mine! See mine!" cried Jeannie as she twisted in the seat to show her back. It was an ad for Coke.

"We found them at the Cancer Aid Thrift Shop," Sally called out, and then she groped again for some way to build a bridge with her mate. The memory of their day at White Cloud and their strange encounter with the two joggers came alive again with a curious new direction.

"Mike, have you tried at all to get in touch with Josh and Sophie?" She was sure he had the little calling card tucked away in his wallet. She hoped she could find a clue to the direction of his thinking.

His answer came slowly. "I wanted to. But I couldn't find the card with their number. I think I left it on my bureau at home."

On the bureau? Sally groaned to herself. To Mike she complained, "I didn't see the card. Did you maybe slip it into a drawer?" He gave no answer but called out new directions as she drove.

"Take a right. That'll head us straight to the Fairgrounds."

Tad spoke up. "Daddy, do you want my playing cards?"

Mike chuckled. "Thanks for the offer, Son, but we're talking about a different kind of card. Maybe when you get home you can give some to Mommy. Turn in here, Sal. The circus will be directly ahead."

Sally had to cope with new worry, that the calling card had been lost forever. After the Toyota settled into a spot in the parking lot, she watched as Mike took each of the children by the hand and piloted their way through the ticket gate and into the crowds of the main enclosure. She was fascinated at his new style of playing the role of father, so different from months past. He paused with them in front of the lion cage, and they were plainly awed by the sleek reality that was pacing back and forth in front of them.

"That's just like on TV!" cried Tad.

Sally had a strong negative feeling about caged animals. She wished they could all be set free to roam nature as was their birthright. Circuses were not a source of entertainment for her.

Mike laid a gentle hand on Tad's shoulder. "Did you know that a lion belongs to the same family as our Fluffy? They're both cats."

The jangling noises of the circus world gradually softened for Sally as she tried to calm the restless tiger within and follow along past the elephant enclosure. Mike led the way. They paused in front of the platform where a juggler performed his skills. Sally noticed, at the front entrance of a tent that housed the side-shows, a pair of clowns cavorting, making light of everyone who passed by, screwing up their faces into all sorts of comic expressions. She grinned in spite of herself.

Mike led on to where they could watch the ferris wheel and then beyond to the merry-go-round. She nodded as he appealed for her permission. "I think this is a safe one. Shall we let the kids try their skills? Okay?"

She was agreeable and moved with him to stand in line at the ticket window. "Do you have enough money?" she asked automatically. "I mean, you did send a lot to help." Her question trailed off leaving unspoken her painful and well known needs back in Grass Valley.

"I got paid again yesterday. We'll be all right."

"Don't you think we should ride with the kids?" She worried about the danger of their falling off. "After all this is a first."

He bought tickets for all four of them and led the way to climb on the gaudy carousel. Sally helped Jeannie mount one of the stationary horses. She wrapped the strap around her waist and stood close to be sure she kept her balance. She watched as Mike helped Tad climb onto one of the prancing thoroughbreds.

The music began, and the huge turntable started its slow turning. Jeannie grabbed the brass pole in front of her saddle, and for the first couple of rotations grew tense as the blurred and scary surroundings flashed by. But gradually, as Sally held firm, Jeannie began to squeal with delight. Up ahead Tad was playing the whooping cowboy on his galloping steed.

At long last when the merry-go-round slowed to its stop Mike helped Sally lead the children as they climbed down from their perch and onto solid ground.

"Can we go again, Daddy?" cried Tad. "Please!"

And Jeannie jumped up and down in excited agreement.

"Please! Please! Please!"

Sally nodded silently to Mike's questioning eyes.

He spoke to the children. "Okay. But this time can

you go without Mom and me holding on to you? Okay?"

He bought the tickets and they helped the children mount their steeds. Together they adjusted the straps and then backed off the platform as it began its whirling journey. They stood watching a dozen paces back and waved as the children came around with their first circuit, slowly speeding up.

Sally watched Mike where he stood several paces closer to the carousel, more than a couple of arm's length distance from her. She didn't feel easy about coming close to him.

Dozens of people, couples and families, were moving past them in search of entertainment. She wished they themselves could be a genuine family once again, linking arms and lives the way she could see people everywhere doing the better way.

And then around the right side of the big rotating plaything she saw the two clowns again. They were jousting with each other in playful comedy, pausing momentarily in front of a family of circus visitors to bow and to scrape and pretend they were doing homage to a king and queen.

With the scene completed, the clowns linked arms with each other, zigging and zagging among the scattered clusters of people. They marched boldly toward where she and Mike stood, and Sally felt an urge to escape rise up in her solar plexus. Were they going to play the fools directly in front of them? She noticed especially that the costume of one was dominantly red while the other was green, and she suspected, although she wasn't sure, at first, that the second one was female.

The entertaining couple came to an abrupt halt, stood between her and Mike and unhooked their arms. The green clown waved her hands wildly at each of them and threw out a bold question. "Are you two related?"

For Sally the words struck as a challenge and awakened all the burden of doubt that nagged her days. She peeked quickly at Mike and then answered as well as she could. "Yes. We're related." She hesitated. "We're married."

The red clown whirled around in an impromptu dance. "Married, hey? And are you having fun being married?"

Sally watched Mike as he made a wry face, shook his head and answered reluctantly. "No. Not really." She was shocked that he would speak so to complete strangers.

"Your honesty is delightful," cried the Green. "So, why don't you get off the MARRY-go-round if it's no fun anymore?"

Sally turned instantly defensive. "Do you mean divorce?" She hadn't intended to let any such language escape her lips, but this was the ultimate threat and her inner protest burst forth in spite of her guard. But at the same time there had been something warmly encouraging in the voice of the jokester, and Sally actually wanted to let the words come into the light of day.

Green clapped her hands together. "Not at all! Not divorce! What I meant was: get off the idea that marriage is ***supposed to be*** *'fun,'* which is what an awful lot of Americans think."

The two clowns grabbed each other's hands and danced around in circles in the jolliest of gestures until Red stopped abruptly, came close and whispered, as though not wanting to be heard by whoever was the proprietor of the circus, "Yes! You should get off the carousel and get with the truly joyful way of making a marriage."

Green stepped near and pushed her face within a foot of Mike's. With thumbs at the side of her head and hands flapping like donkey's ears she declared bluntly, "You two strike us as strangers to each other. How long have you been married?"

"About seven years," Mike answered half-heartedly and leaned back a bit to escape the painted face.

Sally watched uneasily as other circus visitors walking past would stop to observe the comedy. But none of them stayed for long. They soon left to continue toward their own destinations.

"So how old were you," Red demanded of Mike, "when you got married?" He pranced as though he was on the back of a steed of some kind.

"We were eighteen," said Mike, and Sally thought his tone of voice was sullen.

In the background behind the clowns she caught a glimpse of Tad and Jeannie fleeting by on the carousel.

Red pressed hard against Mike. "And how long did it take you to fall out of love?"

Sally flinched at the words, for they shouted what she feared was the final truth.

Mike became surprisingly joyful. "What makes you think I did?" He turned his head toward Sally and spoke softly. "I still love you." His eyes and voice were filled with longing. "I still do. I always will!"

Red and Green grabbed hands and jumped up and down and sang in comic joy, "They're in love! They're in love!"

Green stepped close to Sally and whispered, "Those were the words of a stranger, those words from your man. Weren't they? Love from a stranger! You don't know who he really is, do you?"

She had to nod her head in agreement as she stared at Mike. "No, I don't know who he is." But she was awed by the loving look he had given her and the beautiful words he had spoken.

Red and Green embraced each other for an instant and then chanted in chorus. "Now you have the best possible chance for a new beginning."

Green continued the message. "Everybody at last is a stranger. No one should ever take-for-granted that they 'know' another person. Each one is a truly awesome individual with unique secrets waiting to be discovered."

Sally continued to stare at Mike, and feelings long buried under the rubble of daily life began to break out of their hiding place. She really did love Mike.

Together Red and Green danced a circle around the stunned two-some. Suddenly they stopped and took turns at prodding with the same words. "Go ahead! You can kiss each other! Go ahead! Now!"

As Mike and Sally delayed, Green prodded even harder.

"Here is your beloved stranger! So now is the time to kiss and make up!"

Slowly, almost as though in a common trance, Sally and Mike stepped close. He took her in his arms, and joined her in a deep embrace. For Sally it was like the melting of the polar ice cap. All the glacial slowness of the endless months past became a free-flowing river again. She clung hard to her mate and buried her face in his neck.

When they finally surfaced, Sally turned, wanting to thank the clowns for their loving concern, but the couple had vanished. She and Mike looked toward the merry-go-round as it was slowing down for the end of its run, and there were the colorful pair in the act of swinging on-board just where Tad and Jeannie were riding. The carousel took them out of sight to the opposite side.

Sally was determined to contact them when they would again come around, and she pulled Mike by the hand to step close to the turning platform. It slowed to a stop just where the children were mounted on their steeds, but the clowns were not with them. They had disappeared. The parents climbed on board to release the straps, and Sally looked everywhere, groping for some clue to the missing couple.

Mike reached again for Sally's hand as they stepped down to the ground. She looked into his eyes and knew without words that they shared the same thought. This whole encounter with the strange clowns was so similar to their meeting with the joggers, Josh and Sophie, at White Cloud. What was going on?

As Sally reached for Jeannie, Mike focused attention on Tad as he tugged at the hip pocket of his jeans.

"Daddy, the clown stuck something in here. I can't get it out."

Mike knelt down to be helpful, but he was too late. Tad succeeded. "Wait. I got it."

Sally joined father and son and helped Tad examine the tiny piece of white cardboard. It was bent and smudged.

Mike cried eagerly, "Is it what I think it is?"

Sally answered as she rose to her feet. "It's another

calling card! Look! Here is their phone number again." She turned the card over. Together she and Mike read the message.

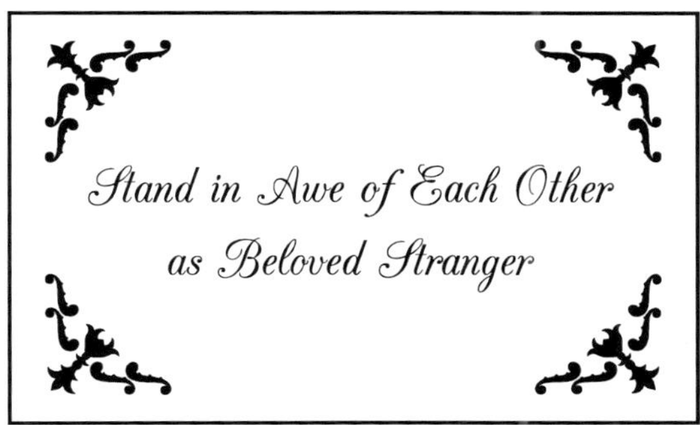

Tears began to creep into her eyelids and she threw her arms around her man and kissed him.

"We found them again!" said Mike.

"Correction," she murmured, grinning joyfully as she whispered in his ear, "They found us!"

Samoa Dunes

The weekend phone calls between Eureka and Grass Valley steadily matured as Sally and Mike worked at listening to the stranger at the other end of the line. Sally's heart warmed with relief as he cheerfully accepted her rambling analysis of Tad and Jeannie's quarreling.

"They fight over the smallest things, like who's getting the biggest piece of melon. Maybe it's just a part of their growing up. Or sometimes I wonder if they are still fussing over our separate households. But there's more to it than that. Until I have to shut them up, and..."

Her experience at Christmas time, when he took the bus home for the holidays, became an oasis of fun in the midst of their desert of separation. She watched with delight as Mike made the most of their tightest of budgets. He brought for the children simple but creative gifts: a checkers game, a doll, a pair of sweaters that were exactly the right size. But as Sally sat in front of the glowing fireplace she questioned to herself, "Are we really on the way to becoming a family?"

On January tenth, a mid-week evening, the Lidster Avenue phone rang, and when Sally found Mike on the other end calling from Eureka her anxiety level moved up a notch. "Is something wrong?"

"No. Not really. I just felt the need to contact home base. Are the children okay?"

Almost in a spirit of routine recitation Sally dutifully reeled off her answer. "Tad loves his first grade. Jeannie brings home cute drawings from kindergarten." This was not what she wanted to talk about. Her inner voice pushed for a different exchange. "But something is new with you, isn't it? I can hear it in your voice."

"Yeah. Something new."

She was puzzled by his flat tone. "Is it bad?"

"Hard to say. I got promoted into the office. I'm an assistant to the sales manager."

"Does that mean more income for us?" Always and always this was the measure of whether they could fight their way out of debt.

"Just a little," he muttered. "Not very much."

"But what's the problem?" There was definitely more that he was holding back.

"I'm not sure yet. You remember how I told you I was beginning to feel that maybe all logging should be stopped?"

"Yes." The shadowed pain of his whistle blowing was still there to pinch at her heart.

"Well, this new job rubs my nose smack in the middle of the problem."

"Are they setting you up for another confrontation?"

He stalled for a minute. "Doubt it. But all this makes me wish I could get more education. Maybe I should try for some correspondence courses."

That was the substantial end to their talk; nothing new at all. When Sally returned the phone to its cradle she felt an ancient guilt perched on her shoulder. It was the same old story. Seven years ago Mike signed up to attend Sierra Community College. Then his lover got pregnant. They had to get married. He had to go to work. He tried a correspondence course. Very thin. Didn't lead anywhere. She felt herself groping against a new frontier.

By the early part of March, Sally's phone jingled again on a mid-week evening, and immediately the tone of Mike's voice shouted "trouble."

"Sal, I'm not the guy for this job. My heart says protect the environment, don't consume it!"

"I've been afraid," said Sally, "ever since you started. I agree." She paused for a second to make sure her feet were on solid ground. "I think we have two possible choices. Quit and come home. Or call Josh and Sophie for their counsel."

After she made a very slow count to ten, Mike's answer came softly. "Yeah. I like that. 'We' have the choice." After another long pause, "I'm not quitting—-yet."

"Well then, let's call our friends. Do you have the calling card with the number?"

"I do. It's really beat up, traveling around in my hip pocket. Here's the number. All right, let's go for it. A conference call. You hang up and I'll start the connection."

Sally wished they were in the same room. She yearned to put an arm around his shoulder in loving support. He was struggling to help his family and nothing was working out. In less than a minute her phone rang and a familiar voice sounded in the receiver.

"Hello. This is Josh. Can we help you?"

Sally held her breath, waiting for her man to pick up the thread and spin out their story.

"Yes. This is Mike, and I..."

"Yes, Mike. Glad to hear from you. Sophie is already on the other line."

"Hello, Mike." It was Sophie's sweet feminine voice. "What can we do for you?"

Sally knew that all of Mike's self-reliant masculine habits of a life time would try to block him from asking for help. Not once in all their years together had he yielded his role as head of the family. But now to her surprise he took the leap.

"I need advice. This new job I have in the office of the Northwest Lumber Company is driving me crazy. I don't know what to do."

"That sounds sort of familiar," said Josh. "You feel you are serving interests which you believe are harmful?"

"Yes. Exactly."

Sophie spoke up. "And at the same time do you feel that you cannot quit because your family needs the income? Sally and Tad and Jeannie are depending on you."

"My thoughts precisely."

Sally rejoiced at the bold, open way her man was managing their problem.

"Mike!" It was Josh speaking with strong encouragement. "We have one central question. What is it in life that you want most?"

Sally kept her silence. Mike had not talked about this question for many months.

"All right," he said at last, "what I want most is the welfare of my family, but I know I cannot have that without the welfare of Planet Earth. That's just the way I feel about it."

Sally found a powerful feeling of awe rise in her soul. She wanted to cheer for what Mike was putting at the top of his values in life.

"Your words are incisive," said Sophie. "What I hear you saying is that you would really want to work in the 'environmental movement.' Is that correct?"

"Yes. That's what I'm getting at. But I don't have the proper education. And..."

Josh interrupted. "It's important that we keep in touch on this matter, Mike. We will need more time to work out the details. So, while we are making appropriate contacts we encourage you to continue at your job and sign up for some correspondence courses. We will get back to you again. Okay?"

Sally continued her silence, for she could feel Mike's disappointment. His "Okay"—-the accepting of their postponement of anything immediately helpful was a hollow echoing of Josh's promise. He hung up the phone and left her with dial tone. She wondered if he would call her back to discuss the emptiness of their contact. He didn't.

On the following day Sally arrived home from a dress-fitting appointment and checked their telephone answering device as it blinked its red light. The message was cryptic. "Please call 272-1662." No doubt, she thought, this was another commercial pitch trying to get through the voice-mail screening barrier. She turned her attention to washing the breakfast dishes and preparing for Jeannie to arrive home from kindergarten.

Her meditation returned again to their big problem. How could she help Mike get back on the college track? Recent dress jobs drove the realization more than ever that her sewing profession at its present level could not support the family. Her stack of original sketches for new costumes still languished on the closet shelf. Even with two other helpers doing the detail work, she would, as a designer, need to break through into a larger market.

Maybe— maybe, she should try, on her own, to call Josh and Sophie. They were definitely the best counselors she could ask for. What was their number?

Suddenly it struck her. The voice mail! Was that their number? She abandoned her post at the kitchen sink, ran to the phone and punched in the number. There was an immediate answer.

"Hello Sally. Glad you called back. This is Sophie. How can we help you?"

Sally found it hard to pull her thoughts into shape. Was this Sophie the jogger? Or Sophie the clown? Or someone else? She rushed on to her big question. How should she tell about the family problem?

"Yes— yes. This is Sally. —I was so glad—so glad you nudged me to call."

"We're pleased, Sally. Josh is here too."

"Hello, Sally. Tell us what's on your mind."

What's on my mind, she thought. *Oh! God help me!* She pulled herself together and spoke with all the steadiness she could muster. "Our marriage and our family is still on shaky ground. We don't have enough income. We're still in debt. And Mike hates his job. And I can feel that he's going to quit. And I believe what he needs is to go back to school. And what we need is..." She trailed off into vagueness because she knew she didn't have the answer.

Josh picked up the thread of her thought. "What you need, it appears, is some way for *you* to earn more, so that Mike could prepare himself for a career he would really enjoy."

"Yes. That's it!" She spoke with rising eagerness. "I'd love to be able to help in that way. I want Mike to be happy!"

Sophie, in her gentle musical voice, joined in on the problem. "Well, perhaps we can direct you to a specific opportunity that would fill your need. You have been an excellent dress designer, but the 'Sally' labels you have put on the garments you create, so far, have not been seen by the right people."

Josh stepped in with a question. "Have you heard of the national dress company called 'Venture'?"

"Oh, yes. It's one of the big ones."

"Well, it just so happens that a vice president of the outfit is visiting his mother in Nevada City. You should call him. —Do you have a pencil? —The number is 265-9357. Ask for George Carlson."

Venture Dress Co.? The sudden rush of excitement that comes with the unlocking of long-closed doors swept through Sally's being. She had known about Venture for many years. Any kind of contact would be awesome. Wow!

Sophie added the final word. "And get that stack of drawings off the closet shelf, pronto."

Sally sat in quiet wonder over the creative ingenuity and know-how of these mentors, and then the front door banged open and Jeannie came bounding in.

"Mommy, Mommy! Guess what!"

The wildness of her little girl pushed Sally to the threshold of painful impatience, but she used restraint and listened.

"What, dear?"

A new girl came to our class today, and she sits right beside me. Her name is Jan."

"Jan and Jean. That's a nice pair."

"She told me they came from San Francisco. They're hunting for a house to live in."

Sally wrapped arms around Jeannie and then whispered, "Well, why don't you tell her about the one across the street. It just went on the market."

She had no way of knowing at that time that her suggestion would change the course of life for the whole family. She was tensed up to take the next step in her dressmaking career and eager to dial the new number.

"Now, Sweetheart, can you run outside and play? I have some more phoning to do."

But the little one had other things on her mind, like a trip to the refrigerator for a sip of apple juice, and a clamor for cookies. It took twenty minutes to clear the deck.

When at last Sally was alone she tried the number. An elderly female voice came on the line. Cautiously Sally asked for permission to speak to George Carlson.

"Carlson, here," was the gruff introduction at last and it increased Sally's tension.

After she presented herself as a dress designer in search of work, she asked the key question. "By any chance have you ever seen the 'Sally' label?"

Gruffness suddenly changed. "'Sally' label? Yes. I've seen several. They're excellent. Yours?"

"Yes," said Sally.

He cleared his throat and spoke cautiously. "I've been wishing for a way to contact you. But no one could give me a good address. Are you available?"

"Oh, yes. I'd be glad to talk with you."

She held in tight rein her amazement at the quiet enthusiasm of the stranger and arranged for him to come to the Lidster Avenue house the next morning.

Sally found George Carlson to be a classically efficient businessman. Even his carefully combed hair and his neatly pressed suit sang the same song. "Business."

He didn't waste a minute with personal matters. He spied the table in the living room loaded with dress sketches and quickly surveyed the whole display.

"Excellent!" was his quick judgment. "This is the kind of work our Sacramento office has been looking for."

"Thank you," said Sally with growing excitement. "I've been wishing I could find a company that would take them on."

"I'll be back in the office tomorrow. If you can let me take some of these drawings along, I'm sure I can get agreement to hire you. For a beginning how would thirty-five thousand a year sound to you?"

For Sally all doubt flew out the window. This was the answer to her prayers. She could make enough money to support the family. She could work at home. She could do what she loved doing. But when at last she was alone again, she thought about Mr. Carlson. One hundred percent business. She felt a touch of uneasiness that he asked not a single word about her personal life and family.

In spite of this, three days later she drove to Sacramento in their aging Toyota and gleefully signed her first contract with VVenture Dress Company.

Sally kept silent about the new enterprise in the presence of the children, and she spoke not a word to Mike during their weekly phone contacts. The stakes were far too big. *I just can't tell him yet. I need time to fit into the job. Maybe when I can show him the money I'm pulling in he'll change his mind. Our whole future could be canceled if he chose to stonewall this opportunity.* But along with her secrecy she managed to work at a growing intimacy between them: friendliness, good cheer, hope.

On the last day of April, after six weeks of relating to her new job, Sally persuaded Grandma to come up from Oakland to baby-sit. This Eureka trip was to be the first in more than two months. She mused on strategy. Should she tell all, right away? Or should she play it cool and let him dig it out of her. She decided not to phone ahead to tell him she was coming. Their recent talks had showed him more discouraged than ever. He needed a joyful surprise. Her final scheme was to arrive late Friday and to be waiting for him when he came home from work. She would wait in his room, which he never locked, for there was nothing anyone would ever want to take.

As she cruised north alone on 101 she mused grimly on how, during the winter months, they had agreed to omit several of her journeys. Saving money was something they both agreed on, and she especially, for with her new world of business she was eager to accumulate more capital. But both of them were hungering because of the postponement of time in bed together.

Carefully she parked the Toyota around the corner where it would not tip him off. She climbed the stairs to his second floor room. It was definitely simple. A double bed. One arm chair. A small bureau. A floor lamp. And a closet. She waited.

In fact she had to wait without supper until past eight

o'clock, for he did not arrive at the five o'clock hour she had reason to expect. She dismissed the fleeting thought that he might be having a date with another woman. It just didn't fit Mike anymore. Her growing restlessness drove her out of the room and down the stairs to the front porch to scan the street, now increasingly shadowed by the onset of night.

At eight-thirty she was sitting on the edge of the bed with the floor lamp glowing when a hand on the doorknob jolted her out of deepening anxiety.

"Sally! When did you arrive?" He rushed to where she sat and dropped onto the bed beside her. He planted a kiss and the warmest hug she could wish for. "Why didn't you tell me your were coming?"

His ardor pushed back the tears that lurked in the near background. "I got here at four o'clock," she moaned.

"Oh, my darling! You should have phoned. The boss took us out to dinner. You could have been there with us."

"The best laid plans of mice and woe-men..." A deep sigh of relief took Sally back toward normalcy. "I wanted to surprise you."

"Well," chortled Mike, "you have brought me the most wonderful surprise of all. You!" He moved up onto the bed and took her into his arms with a rising passion that awakened hers. Swiftly Sally let go of all her plots and plans and joined him in a happy return to love making. Before the hour was out they came up from the depths panting and rejoicing.

Mike whispered into her ear, "That was the best sex we've had in a long time."

"You have also answered my hunger for supper," she crooned. "I'm completely satisfied."

In deep contentment they lay in close embrace until sleep took over, and Sally found comfort in leaving to the morrow all of the giant problems that had brought her to Eureka.

On Saturday morning, with the weather in its normal foggy springtime mode, and after a brief boarding-house breakfast, they sat side by side in the porch swing. Sally took Mike's hand in hers hoping to move them closer to the moment of truth. Suddenly he became aware of the puzzle of the missing car.

He spoke with rising anxiety. “Where’s the Toyota?”

“Nobody has stolen it,” Sally chuckled. “Part of my surprise. I parked it around the corner.”

“Okay,” he muttered, “so life is full of surprises. How about telling me the rest of your surprises. Why did you sneak up on my blind side?”

“Not so fast,” Sally answered, patting him on the cheek. “Some other things come first. Like, tell me about your job. How do you feel about it now?” She looked deep into his eyes.

Mike turned away and fell silent for a spell. “At dinner last night my boss tried to present himself as an environmentalist. But he failed completely. There was no mistake that for him only one thing mattered. The bottom line. It made me sick to my stomach.”

“Does your correspondence course give you any help?” She probed for more clues.

“Not a lot. The thing I really need to go for is a degree. But you know...” His voice trailed off into helpless silence.

“Don’t you think,” said Sally, groping for a path that could take her safely to the destination she held in secret, “don’t you think we should get some help on this?”

“Like what?”

“We could try calling Josh and Sophie. They have been good counselors to us.”

“Hey, it’s useless.” There was a deeply sour tone to Mike’s response. “We tried calling them more than six weeks ago. They promised to call back. I haven’t heard a squeak.”

“Maybe we should try again.” Sally wasn’t about to quit the path they had laid out.

“Look. The bottom line for us is still the same. I’ve got to stick with this job to keep a roof over the heads of the people I love.”

His intensity and his loyalty and his masculine determination deepened Sally’s fear that he would totally reject any plan that would put her in the driver’s seat as breadwinner. After a heavy silence, grasping for a last straw, she became bold far beyond her habit. She spoke with decisively clipped speech.

"Well, I think we should ask for help. It certainly won't hurt to try calling our mentors again. I'll go down stairs to the pay phone in the hallway. Have you got a quarter I could use?" She reached out her hand.

"Now?" Mike stared at her with doubt and resistance.

"Yes. Now. May I have it, please?" She was firm.

He could hardly refuse. He dug in his pocket and handed her the coin. She grabbed his hand and led the way to the lower floor. She punched in the number. Immediately the familiar voice came on line. "Hello. Sophie speaking. How can we help you?"

Sally flashed a quick glance at Mike and winked affectionately at him as she answered. "It's Sally and Mike again. We need your help."

"Of course." It was the voice of Josh. "How about we get together? Can you come to the ocean beach beyond the Samoa Dunes?"

Sally turned quickly to Mike. "Do you know where the Samoa Dunes are?"

"Sure. Been there a couple of times."

Sally returned to the phone, "Yes. We'll be glad to."

Abruptly the phone went silent, and Sally exulted to Mike, "They want us to come to the beach beyond the dunes."

"Guess that'll be okay. Will they be waiting for us?"

"I assume so. That was the idea."

"Right now?"

"I think so." She realized the instructions had been very cryptic. She wondered if their sudden cut off was troubling Mike.

As they swung around the corner to where the Toyota was parked, Sally dug into her purse that hung by a strap over one shoulder.

"Here are the keys, Mike. Would you drive, please?"

She wanted him to find comfort in what was now a modest leadership role. He steered their car over the bridge that crossed Indian Island and the Humboldt Bay inlet until they came to the New Navy Base Road. The highway turned south along the Pacific Coast beach, and then swung to the east side along the inlet. Toward the southern end of the peninsula he found a place to park on a spur road.

"Here are the Samoa Dunes," he declared. "It's going to be quite a hike out to the beach.

Sally felt the oppression of the overhead fog that dominated the Eureka weather. A steady breeze washed their faces as they climbed over one dune after another. At last they caught sight of the beach and the breakers pounding in across the deserted sands. There was not another soul in sight. No Josh no Sophie.

As they trotted down to the edge of the water, Sally found herself pulled into a mood of wonder at the primitive reality of the boundless ocean. The crashing surf filled her with delight and awe. Mike scanned the beach to the north and the south.

"Well, where are they?" His tone told of the growing skepticism that had possessed him.

"I don't know," said Sally. "They didn't set a time. Sophie just said to come to the beach beyond the dunes. I guess we'll just have to wait. Anyway, it's a beautiful day," she exalted, trying to put on the most cheerful aspect possible.

"Yeah," said Mike accepting her positive gesture as the best they could do. "It's a wonderful beach. Unbroken. From the tip of the peninsula, all the way up to Crescent City. I love it. Let's walk. Come on."

"I'm going to take off my shoes and wade in the water," said Sally, and she sat on the damp sand among the fragments of drying kelp that were strewn everywhere. Mike didn't need any encouragement to follow suit.

As she wriggled her bare toes deeper into the cool beach surface with her unique beloved "strange" man sitting close beside her, she realized that the light of love was shining powerfully from his otherwise gray eyes of despair over the hopeless state of the world environment.

They walked south to the tip of the peninsula. They walked north, and nowhere did they see any signs of the people they were supposed to meet. The beach was abandoned, except at one remote spot where a mother and three children were playing in the sand at the northern end of their walk.

After more than two hours, when the dim sun could be guessed at as approaching the zenith, Sally realized with deep unease that she could no longer hold back the secret business of her trip to Eureka. Time was running out. She had to make the case.

With her feet being washed by the salty surf and Mike by her side she reached into her purse and pulled out a fat manila envelope and handed it to her husband.

"Take a look inside," she said.

He received the offering with a puzzled look spreading across his face. He sprung open the metal clasp. From the inside he pulled out a packet of greenbacks held together by a pair of rubber bands. They were twenty-dollar bills. Silently he began counting. There were fifty of them. He turned to stare at Sally.

"What's up? Did you play the lottery?"

"No, Mike. Don't be silly. For six weeks I have been working at a new job with Venture Dress Company. This is the surplus after all our bills were paid."

"No. This is not good."

"But Mike, my working at this kind of job will make it possible for you to come home and enroll full-time at Sierra College." She poured out her story in a flood of eagerness. "Think of it. In two years you could have your A.A. And then you could go on from there. The campus is within walking distance of our house. And the children would love to find you at home part of the time when they come back from their school." Sally would have gone on and on, but Mike shook his head savagely and took half a dozen steps deeper into the oncoming surf.

"No. No. No. It's not right."

The look on his face did not surprise her. It was what she expected and feared. His male stature had been cut down like a fallen redwood tree. He was laid low. As a new breaker sent water washing across their feet he groaned.

Sally's dismay at his habitual patriarchal attitudes

grew swiftly, sliding toward hopelessness.

Mike was about to spill out more negatives. Suddenly he stopped and stared beyond the breakers. Sally followed his gaze. Out of the water a couple of swimmers rose up to their feet and slowly walked toward where they stood. The man was brown-skinned with black hair, strong and muscular. The woman was stunning, with a full head of wet black hair hanging down around her shoulders. She was full-breasted, beautiful and smiling as though the day were full of joy. Could they be latinos? Or what?

Sally came to stand beside her husband and was astounded to see anyone sturdy enough to swim in the chilly waters. And where had they come from? In from the deep, deep ocean? The couple stopped directly in front of them with no signs of discomfort from the wind that dried the dripping water from their bodies.

"We're glad you're here," said the man.

And the woman added, "We didn't want to interfere with your talking to each other, until you were ready."

Sally was overwhelmed. "Ready? I can't—- I don't know how to —- I mean, is it really you?"

Mike was quick to cross the abyss of questionable identity. "Josh and Sophie! That's it, isn't it?"

"Often people see us differently," said Sophie. "And now why don't we get on with the big issue of the day?" She reached out and shook open the manila envelope which Mike still gripped in his hands. "You have quite a stack of bills there."

"Yeah. Money," he grumbled. "Sally is trying to take over the role of provider for the family."

"Do you feel robbed?" said Josh. "Your hand is full of money, but you are resenting it?"

Mike's angry mood was ready to crush all opposition. "But it's my job to—-" Sally yearned to restrain him.

"Hold it for a minute," said Sophie. "Who gave you the task of being the wage earner?"

"Well—- Nobody gave me the task. It's the way everybody does it."

"Not anymore," said Josh. "The American culture has

changed. The old patriarchy is being replaced by something much more creative."

Sally could not hold back. "That's what I'm trying to tell him."

"No!" said Mike, driving to cut her off. "She's telling me she doesn't need me anymore."

"At this point we must be very careful," said Sophie. "Otherwise we'll miss the big picture. The first part is the old question: what after all is the purpose of marriage? Or have you forgotten?"

Mike glanced at Sally by his side and grimaced. "No, I haven't forgotten. The purpose of marriage is to create family, like you taught us."

"And now let's hear the second part. What is family?"

"It's me and Sal and the kids."

"Oh?" said Sophie, pushing harder. "And what else?"

"What do you mean? The family is the family."

"That's a real tiny definition. Four people in the same house? What about relatives? The larger family? And what about planet Earth?"

Josh joined the exchange. "Mike, did you ever look in the dictionary for the root meaning of family?"

"No."

"It comes from the Latin 'famulus', meaning servant. In the days of Rome, of course, that meant the slaves of the household. Today the meaning has matured. 'Family' at last is any bunch of people who serve each other's needs."

"Yeah," Mike broke in quickly, "that's my purpose in life. To serve Sally's and the children's needs."

Again Sophie joined in. "And does that mean that you will refuse to let your wife serve her husband's needs?"

"The point," Sally called out firmly, "the point is that Mike needs to improve his education. And I am ready and willing to serve that need. We both of us need for him to go back to school."

An extra large breaker came pounding onto the beach and washed hard against the legs of all in the group, sucking and moving the sands beneath their feet.

Sally watched Mike's confusion grow deeper, and before

he could protest, Sophie picked up the thread again. "All right, let's go on to the third point. This is the hardest for human beings to understand. You are male and female. Right? How are you going to manage your differences? I don't mean in bed. I mean in every hour of the day as you try to serve each other's needs."

Sally and Mike glanced at each other, groping for a way to come to grips with the problem that had been laid out before them.

Josh made a further contribution. "What Sophie is calling to your attention is that males and females tend to have different natures. You, Sally, tend to be a nurturer, holding together the household scene. You, Mike, see yourself as an explorer, out in the world trying to find the better way to support the homebodies."

Mike didn't hesitate a moment to underline his role. He stepped close to Sally and wrapped an arm around her shoulder. "Right!" he said. "I'm an explorer. And I love her!"

"But there is another point," Sophie continued. "In the family you need to be like a flock of wild geese. In flight there will be one who is the leader of the great V-formation up there in the sky. That's a hard job. The beating of his wings is what breaks up the static air and makes it easier for the rest to follow."

Mike was about to proclaim his agreement, but Sophie held up her hand. "Wait! Hear the finale! In regular fashion the leader finally drops back and lets another member of the 'family' move up to the front to take a turn at leadership. Family is when and where people fill each other's needs. Take turns, Mike. To be a server is sometimes to be a leader and sometimes to let others lead. We'll leave you to take it from there." Her speech was short and final.

She reached out and joined hands with Josh, and without another word they headed back into the breakers. As Sally stood close to Mike in silence, shaken by their sudden departure, they watched the brown-skinned swimmers disappear into the deep. The water continued to wash across their own feet, and their meditation stretched the silence until a break in the clouds overhead let a shaft of sunlight pour down onto their heads.

Sally squirmed loose from Mike's grip and faced him squarely. "Well, Mr. Goose, are you ready to let me have a turn as leader of the flock?" This was the moment of truth.

"Hmm," Mike responded. "I guess maybe Sophie has a point. I do need to go back to school. Who knows how long. But it could make a difference."

"All right. What you have in your hand can be the nest egg to get us started. You will have a turn at being a nurturing homebody, and I will do the best I can at being the explorer."

Mike wrapped his arms around her again and planted a wet kiss. Sally felt it as his real acceptance of the new pattern of life that was shaping up for them.

As they drove back toward the city Mike spoke up with a touch of irony. "There's something different about this visit from our mentors. No calling card."

"That's true. I wonder why?" And then she spoke of her own musings. "I've been thinking how they came to us out of the depths of the ocean. There's got to be something symbolic about that. I mean, that's the most beautiful picture I can imagine. Our whole life is lived on the shore and they bring us the deep stuff."

The first thing Mike did when they were finally back in his room was to pull out of his jacket the manila envelope with its treasure of twenty-dollar bills.

"For sure," he said, "you'll need some of this more than I will." He spread open the flap to dig out the greenbacks. There was a moment of shock. The first thing he found under the rubber band was one of the calling cards. "Look!

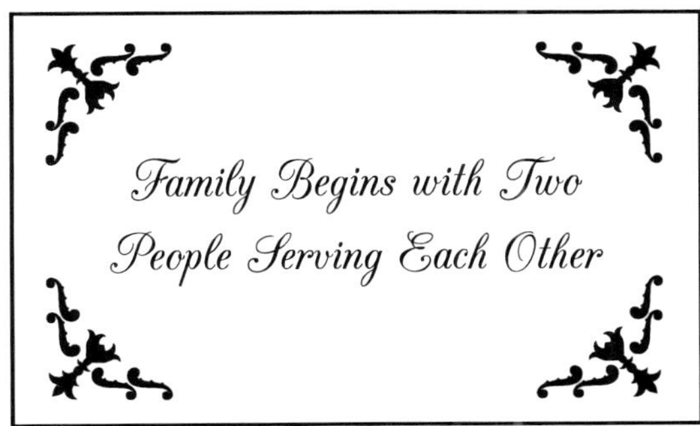

Lidster Avenue

On the last Saturday before Summer Session was to begin at Sierra Community College, Sally and Mike enjoyed a late breakfast. Their hearts were full to overflowing with the promises of their new life: Mike's return to school and her growing dress profession. But the quiet review of plans was sharply interrupted as Tad and Jeannie came racing in from the yard with a quarrel.

"All right, what's the matter this time?" Sally challenged as they positioned themselves on opposite sides of the dining table.

Jeannie's quick complaint focused on the trowel she gripped in her hand. "He tried to take it away from me."

"I was using it first," came Tad's sour response. "She grabbed it when I wasn't looking."

Quietly Mike entered the fray. "Have you ever heard of sharing? Can you two work out some way to take turns?"

Sally's heart sang its new song as she watched her man give strong and practical application to the great principle that was now guiding their adult lives. Take turns! She shoved the children outside again with praise, "You are big kids now. See if you can agree for a change."

When they were gone Mike reached across the table to take her hand in his. "My dear Stranger, I love the way you pass on to the children the lessons we have learned. I'm glad you and I are back on track after so much fumbling."

Sally left her chair and came around the table. With a beaming smile she sat on Mike's lap, and they rejoiced in a loving embrace and kiss.

"You and I may be 'back on track,'" she murmured, "but our off-spring are still 'back in the freight yard.' I think we still have a long way to go. For light years we stumbled along. And look at them. Two kids stuck in the same old rut of competition. Parenting is not our strongest point."

"Hmmm," Mike whispered with a touch of teasing, "are you hinting that there is another piece of leadership that we have to conquer?"

"I'll forgive your choice of words, for the moment. But yes. We have a bigger assignment than we know."

"Well, suppose you outline what the lesson is. Let's talk about parenting."

Sally was not granted the chance. Sharply again a door slammed open, this time the front door. Jeannie came running to their side with wild excitement. Her T-shirt was stained with the dirt of the backyard play pit.

"Mommy, they're moving in across the street. The truck just drove up."

"All right. We knew it would happen sooner or later," said Sally patiently. "Someone was sure to buy."

"But it's Jan. My friend at school!"

"Oh? Are you sure?"

"Come! Come and see!"

Jeannie pulled on Sally's arm and led the parents out to the porch where Tad was watching.

The house across the street was considerably larger than Mike and Sally's modest bungalow. It was a two-story structure filling a much wider lot. The moving van's rear gate was open and workmen were busy untying ropes that held the furniture in place. A young man and woman were standing on the front lawn.

Sally, playing her new role as leader of the flock, found simple words forming naturally on her lips. "Come on. Let's meet them."

Mike, however, was not ready. "We should wait. Give them time to settle in."

Sally wondered why his instincts as explorer were now being denied. Was he dropping back into the role of a conservative follower? She pressed harder.

"I know if I were moving into a new neighborhood I would appreciate being welcomed. Come on!" She grabbed his hand and with the children led the way across the street toward the newcomers. As they crossed the rain-gutters which served as the only sidewalks Lidster Avenue could boast, and drew near the new people she found a strange wordless feeling fill her soul, something about the way the couple were standing, a hunch that this would not be a casual contact. The man was broad-shouldered and muscular; the woman small and stout. Sally became very uneasy and fought to shake off the negative foreshadowing.

The new couple turned to meet the neighbors that came toward them. Sally kept silent and squeezed Mike's hand to urge him to pick up the ball. He caught on and led the way, focusing his greeting on the young man.

"Hello! And welcome to Lidster Avenue."

"Howdy," was the man's answer. "We're the Gordons."

Sally smiled to herself as Jeannie easily drifted over to stand with the girl who obviously must be her classmate. The man pressed on without hesitation. "And I think we have to thank your daughter for telling our Jan that this house was on the market. I'm Bill. This is Irene. And our little one is Andy,"

"I'm Mike, and this is Sally," came the echoing introduction.

Sally found herself pursuing deeper estimates of the newcomers. Bill Gordon was clearly younger than Mike. Maybe five years his junior. But he was big. His shaggy brown hair appeared like a hangover from the nineties. Irene seemed to be nervous and shy and retiring. Pretty, but under stress. Jan was a restless kid, impulsive and energetic. Andy, about four years old, was content to be rolling around on the cool grass.

Abruptly there was a break in the talk. Bill Gordon shouted at the men who were unloading the truck. "Watch out for that gun rack!" As he took a first step closer, Irene laid a hand on his arm in a gesture of restraint, but he shook her off. "Stop that!"

He took another step to where the men were lifting the rack toward the sidewalk. "That's my most valuable piece in the whole move! You break it, I'll have your heads."

The movers showed extreme care as they hefted the rack toward the front door. Bill returned to continue getting acquainted, but Sally, now in retreat, felt the time was not ripe and gave a warning tug on her husband's elbow.

Bill's words were conventional. "It's a great neighborhood. Beautiful street."

"Yes," said Mike, "feels good to be on the hilltop."

He would have gone on but Sally's second tug got to him. "If there's anything we can do to help," he added, "please feel free to call on us." And with that he and Sally took Tad by the hand to return home, leaving Jeannie to play with her neighbor friend.

"And don't get in the way," Sally cautioned.

Once again in their home, Sally began clearing the breakfast table, but she paused with heaviness of spirit. "Mike, did you get a feeling that Mrs. Gordon is a browbeaten wife?"

"Not really. Why do you imagine that?"

"She didn't say a word, and not once did she make eye contact. I couldn't feel that we had really met her."

"But why do you say browbeaten?" Mike pursued. "I would say they are just an average family. Nothing out of the ordinary."

"Well, I'm sorry. I picked up some worrisome vibes. I see Mr. Gordon as big and tough. I think trouble is brewing in that family."

"Huh. That's jumping ahead awfully fast." He stopped in the middle of his clearing the breakfast table, and Sally found herself fascinated by the new look in his eyes. "But now I am wondering what happened to my lead goose? You dropped back and let me take over. What gives?"

As her newly cooperative partner, she kissed him on the cheek without a word, leaving him to find his own answer. Together they made short work of the chores.

The first Monday of June, the opening day of Sierra College classes, dawned with all the beauty of a white-streaked sky framed by the high green horizons of the up-reaching Sierra forests.

After Mike set out to walk the mile to the campus Sally saw the children off to their last week of school and settled down to her drawing board, which now preempted one corner of the living room. Her work had become a magnet of joy that pulled without any resistance from her at all.

Somewhere in mid-morning the doorbell jingled and there stood Irene Gordon and her pre-school Andy.

"Good morning," said Sally, with questioning in her voice, because her new neighbor apparently had no words to explain their presence. "What can I do for you?"

Irene gradually came to focus. Her thoughts took shape slowly. "You were so friendly. When we moved in. On Saturday. We don't know anybody. Up here." For a moment she trailed off into silence. And then she added shyly, "I thought we ought to get better acquainted."

"Of course. Right!" said Sally, uneasy that she had been so slow with her hospitality. "Please come in."

Andy's liveliness became an immediate problem. He left his mother's grip and headed toward the big drawing board in the corner of the living room. Sally was not about to let the invader have his choice and quickly moved to take his hand and lead to a new opportunity.

"Come over here, Andy. In this closet we have some real goodies." She opened the door and with his help dragged out a large box of building blocks, which they dumped in the middle of the carpet. Her ploy worked perfectly.

When at last Sally could sit with Irene on the sofa she opened the way to new conversation. "Did I understand correctly that you come from San Francisco?"

"It isn't a good place for kids. We were having more and more troubles." Irene seemed stiff where she sat with her hands gripping each other and her gaze fixed on her boy at his play.

"The big city can be tough," Sally agreed, hoping her expression of interest would open more doors.

"Jan was always getting into trouble," Irene added.

Sally guessed that their trouble had little to do with San Francisco and more with fumbling parenthood. "Do you mind if I ask a personal question?"

"Whatever," said Irene without resistance.

"How old are you?" She made it feel as friendly as she could.

"I'm twenty-one. Bill's twenty-two." She turned to look her hostess directly in the eyes.

"I see." Sally hesitated. "And your daughter Jan is six?"

Without blinking Irene let the truth be known. She seemed relieved to be sharing the facts of their life. "I was barely fifteen." She pressed on. "When Bill knew that I was pregnant he insisted that we live together. He was totally against abortion. He wanted kids. That was very important for him."

"Well," Sally pressed on supportively, "I imagine you've had some pretty hard times. Two children can be a big challenge!"

"The hardest part is the way Bill disciplines them." Her hands became very expressive as they reached toward Sally in a gesture of open appeal. "When he sees them misbehave he whips hard. It makes me cry along with them."

"I'm sorry to hear that." Sally sensed that Irene had major problems of her own with her husband, but she put a strong foot on the brake when it came to asking about those details. She found her sympathies reaching out, wishing that she might somehow bring a touch of peace to this newcomer in her life.

Their talk went on for the remaining time of the morning and was interrupted at last when the school bus was scheduled to drop off Jeannie and Jan. Irene excused herself with a grateful hug, which she delivered to Sally with a whispered farewell. "Thank you so much for listening to me."

At bedtime Sally and Mike found precious moments to share the events of their day and quickly discovered the major focus was on the Gordons.

"Yeah," said Mike, "I found Bill walking just ahead of me, on the way to the campus. I caught up with him, and we talked. He also is going for his A.A. degree."

"What a strange coincidence," said Sally. "Both of you. And Bill doesn't have a job either? I wonder how they manage."

"Bill's dad is a San Francisco broker. They'll get a monthly allowance, so long as he stays in school. After I asked him how they managed, he wanted to know about us. I told him about your job with Venture." Mike chuckled. "His reaction showed me more about him than anything yet. He sneered. He said, 'So you let your wife run the show?'"

"Oh, Mike! That's terrible! I'm not 'running the show'! I'm only taking my turn." For a moment Sally felt all the struggle of the past year come harshly back.

"Cool it, Sweetheart. You don't have to be defensive. Bill's attitude is Bill's. What's more interesting, he's majoring in finance. And I quote. He said, 'I've got to lick the business world.' That told me a lot."

"Like what?" She rolled over to face her man more directly.

"It says we're poles apart. When I let him know I was headed for environmental studies his tone turned to pity. He was sure I was headed for a poverty profession."

Sally mused for a moment. "So it's all right for his father to pay his way in school, but it's not all right for your wife to do the same?"

"Yep. That's Bill. He's really a hard driver. But I can't help liking him anyway."

The stresses of the day finally caught up with them and they drifted off into sleep. And in the days that followed, because her ears were attuned, Sally began to keep score using a little note pad on her drawing board to total up the number of times she overheard screaming or shouting or tears from the kids across the street and from their mother.

As the weeks wore on the stories she and Mike shared took on greater and greater intensity. Clearly the neighbor family was not functioning smoothly at all.

Sally at last was moved to put her feelings into words. "You know, sometimes I even wonder if they can properly be called a family."

"What do you mean? That's harsh."

"Well, you know what Sophie and Josh taught us. A

family is two or more people serving each other's needs. The Gordons don't fit. I'm sensing that Bill has three slaves who serve only him."

"Hmmm. That's about the worst thing you can say. I don't know if I can go along with that. But I can agree, Bill is a driver."

By the middle of the summer Sally found that the Gordon family distractions were seriously interfering with her work for Venture Dress. She had launched her job with the high joy of creativity, but now there was also the pain of meeting deadlines. Her boss, Mr. Carlson, insisted that she have a group of designs delivered by July 31st. There were simply not enough hours in the day.

She had to cope with Tad and Jeannie quarreling, on top of the hours spent with wounded Irene, and checking on Jeannie's roamings with Jan, and Mike's reports about Bill.

When it was all over she cried out to Mike in her exhaustion. "I can't hack it. My neck is killing me. I'm practically in the same bad shape as when we went up to White Cloud."

"Come here," he proposed, "and sit in the chair, and let me give you a massage." He practiced his role of being the nurturer.

She cooperated silently as he worked on the tensed muscles, and then she groaned, "I've got to slow down on being Irene's confidante."

"Glad to hear you say that," said Mike. "I was about to insist on exactly the same. How about scheduling her time with you? Like 2 p.m. twice a week?"

"Yes. Yes." Her tone was not at all convincing.

His voice took on the character of a drill sergeant. "That's what a parent would do with her wounded child. Talk about good intentions. Just do it!"

Sally responded slyly. "You wouldn't be falling into the role of dominator, would you?"

Mike laughed. "Hah. Being married to one's favorite wife isn't the simplest thing in the world."

When at last the college summer session came to its

end, Mike had to admit that Sally was right that there was a spreading gulf in life-style between themselves and the Gordons. Their best hour for talking about the day was still bedtime. As they lay side by side in their big bed, with only a sheet to cover them during the hot night, Mike reeled out his discoveries.

"Bill confided to me that his father provided the full purchase price for their home. $250,000! But that's not what he spent it for. He made a down payment of 50 thou. The rest of it he used to get into the stock market."

"Oh," said Sally, "that's terrible." Here was more of their hidden world she had sensed from the beginning. "Does his father know?"

"Complete secret. But here is the payoff. Bill is so sharp, picking up clues on the Internet, and probably everywhere else, that in just two months he has doubled his investment. He says now he can retire the mortgage, and he still has big money to continue his spree. I've never had to relate to a guy like that. He's the most aggressive character I've ever met."

Sally's story about her latest contact with Irene was dark. "When she came to see me this afternoon I noticed a purple bruise around her left eye. I had to ask. She dodged. She didn't come right out and admit that Bill had hit her. But she didn't deny it either."

"Ouch," said Mike. "Sounds like a case for the Domestic Violence Coalition."

"I think maybe it's our case," said Sally. "We've gotten in so deep already."

Mike rolled onto his side to face Sally. "I can see you've made some progress with Irene. But I haven't any clue about how to help my friend Bill. He's the tough one."

Sally reached for Mike's hand. "Yeah. I agree. This is much bigger than we know how to deal with. The job is failed parenting, and we're not very great at that ourselves. Do you know what I think? I think we should get on the phone to Josh and Sophie."

In the dim twilight of the bedtime world Mike kissed her. "I think you have a good idea, sweetheart. Let's do just that, the first thing in the morning."

"I have a better idea," she said, tickling his ribs. "Let's do it right now."

Sally flipped back the sheet and groped her way around the bed, guided only by the dim rays of the street lamp filtering through the curtains and onto her bare skin. She returned with their two cell phones, snapped on the bed-side lamp and promptly dialed the now familiar number.

"We have a problem," Sally began.

"Yes," Sophie responded, "we wondered how long it would be before the Gordons' world might shake you up."

Mike voiced his wonderment. "Do you know about them too?"

"We've been following their lives for some time," Josh answered. "They are not a group, as yet, who are able to listen to us. That's why we are counting on you. We want you to keep talking with them."

"But we really don't know where to begin," cried Sally. "Their world is so full of violence. It's almost as though we're talking foreign languages to each other."

"Very true," said Sophie. "It's going to take a lot of time. They're not a family yet. Do you think you can deepen your reservoir of patience as you try to draw them into a family relationship?"

"But it feels like we're at a dead end," said Sally. "We've listened to both of them. They seem ready to unload their pain. Irene does, anyway. But nothing comes of it." All the frustrations of the past weeks came flooding back.

Mike spoke up. "What else is there for us to do? I mean, if you want us to keep close there must be some specific place to start."

Josh's voice came softly through the ear-pieces. "Well, for starters, as you have already observed, the Gordons are almost completely ignorant about their assignment to be good parents to Jan and Andy. So parenting is a very natural place to begin. Bill's a whipper. Irene's a do-nothing mom."

"But we're not very smart parents ourselves," moaned Sally. "I feel like a fumbler most of the time."

"We're glad you can admit that," said Sophie. "You are in the same boat with most of your fellow humans. But your difference is that you really want to do better."

"Wait a minute," cried Mike. "I think Sally has found the truth about the Gordons. She sees them not as family but as a household of slaves; Irene and the kids serving Bill."

Josh spoke up. "This is why we say again, the place to begin is to show them how to become good parents, which is the first step to becoming a family. Do you think you could begin by being good parents to them? Serve their needs? Accept the wounded child in each one? It's the surest way to help them get beyond the marry-go-round. Because without help they're headed for 'broken family' status."

Sally spoke vigorously from where she sat on the edge of the bed. "Hold it. Did I hear clearly? You want us to be parents to these two parents?"

"You heard correctly," said Josh. "Practically every person on planet Earth has a wounded child inside. Accepting, loving, serving the needs of that child is the big assignment. It's what makes family at last."

"What's missing," said Sophie, "is they did not make a commitment to be a family. And by commitment we mean a conscious intention to serve each other's needs. They did not really understand that the foundation of family life is loving service to each other."

"Yes, we know all that," said Mike.

Josh spoke quietly, "Rest assured, we will repeat this principle a thousand times if necessary, until it is heard."

Sally tried again, "I still feel we are stalled."

"Hold it," Mike intervened. "I just remembered something! There was a poster on the bulletin board at the college. It was inviting people to come to a "Class on Parenting" to be held in the Seaman Lodge in Pioneer Park. It's being sponsored by—- I think maybe it was the PTA. I forget the date."

"You can find the date," Josh added, "if you check the announcements in the Union."

"We recommend," said Sophie, "that you do your best to persuade the Gordons to go with you. And be assured we will keep in touch. See you soon!"

With that the phone contact came to an end, and the task of convincing Bill and Irene to attend was launched in the hearts of Sally and Mike.

She checked the Friday newspaper and found that the class of six weeks would begin on the following Tuesday evening. Also she learned from Mike that a psychology professor from whom he had taken a course at Sierra College would be in charge. That helped to expand his motivation to attend and to begin groping for ways to persuade Bill.

Unpredictably the events of the weekend produced extra help. The Toyota broke down on Saturday. It had to be towed to a repair shop on east Main Street, and the diagnosis called for a new transmission, the parts for which could not be ordered until Monday with installation no earlier than Wednesday.

On Sunday afternoon Sally had barely started on the dinner dishes when she spotted Bill busy with mowing their front lawn. She signaled to Mike who was in the backyard watering their small patch of lawn.

"Maybe this is the moment we've been waiting for. Let's check him out."

"Do you want me to do the talking?" said Mike, gently hinting at their competing roles of leadership.

"He won't listen to me," said Sally. "We've seen that a dozen times. I'm no better than Irene. But with you and him it's big masculine togetherness all the way."

Hand in hand they crossed the street and Mike began apologetically. "Bill, we've got a problem, and I wonder if we might count on you for help?"

"Try me and see," was his restless response as he interrupted the work at hand.

"Sally and I are eager to attend a class at Seaman Lodge on Tuesday, but our car is in the repair shop. I just wondered if you could drive us there?"

"Hey, what are friends for? Sure thing."

His brightness ended any further caution. “In fact,” Mike made it sound as after-thought, “maybe you and Irene would like to go with us.” He was playing the eager salesman. “It could be an interesting evening for all four of us.”

“Sounds like fun. So what’s the class about?”

Sally smiled as Mike stretched himself to make the subject matter seem secondary. “One of our profs at the college is in charge. It’ll be stuff about how to improve our parenting skills. You know. It’s something we all need.”

“Yeah. Sure. Well, I’ll put it on the calendar.”

Mike sucked in a breath of relief. “Great.”

Sally thought there was a note of off-handedness in Bill’s acceptance. Apparently he had no blockage about the word parent.

After more pleasantries about the weather and the coming of Fall in a few weeks, they returned home. Sally exulted that the cues of their mentors were working out. She called Mike to help her finish the kitchen sink chore.

“I’ve been thinking a lot about the Gordons,” she declared, and with a smile that was loaded with mystery, she added, “and what about us?”

“About us? What do you mean?” Mike’s eyes opened wider with curiosity.

“With the help of Sophie and Josh you and I have come through some pretty deep waters. Now, if we take our mentors seriously, they are telling us we are to practice parenting with the Gordons. Do you really think we are ready?”

Mike came close and took her into his arms, soapy wet hands and all. “Thank you, darling, for your patient parenting with me. I think we should try with the Gordons.”

Following supper on Tuesday, with a single baby-sitter provided for all four children, Mike and Sally checked in at the Gordon house, with Tad and Jeannie in tow. Irene answered the doorbell. The anguish in her face told Sally immediately that there was trouble inside. They moved into the living room in time to find Bill in the act of disciplining Jan. He was administering a severe spanking to her bared butt, and she was screaming. In a moment it was over and Jan ran sobbing into her bedroom.

"Come on," said Bill. "Let's get out of here."

Sally was in deep sorrow to see the anger in his face. In the car as the two sets of parents headed for class Bill explained. "She's got to learn that I won't stand for her putting on a tantrum when we are going out somewhere."

To herself Sally moaned, treating a weepy tantrum with a spanking tantrum never heals any wound. Sitting with Mike in the back seat they flashed to each other a glance of pain and a secret squeeze of their hands. This was exactly why the Gordons needed the class.

As soon as the car swung onto Ridge Road Bill's foot grew heavy on the accelerator, and Sally held her breath. After each stop sign he pushed their auto more than 20 miles above the speed limit. *Bill the angry driver,* she thought to herself.

They arrived in swift time at Seaman Lodge and Sally took Irene under her wing as they found seats in the assembly room. She guessed there were as many as two dozen who had turned out. Mike sat in the second row next to her and Irene, with Bill holding down a seat by the aisle.

Professor Hank Martin, a candidate for retirement, began with a formal introduction, which rambled on in generalities that left his audience groping for some way to take hold. The gist of his comments were too familiar.

"American society during the past century has done some strange things with the ancient institution of marriage and family, as you all know. With the steady failure of parenting, juvenile crime and violence has risen to terrifying extremes. Our prisons are more severely crowded than those of any other nation on the planet...."

Suddenly he interrupted his rambling and stared at the audience. "Incidentally, how many of you are married?" He raised his right hand, inviting the group to answer.

Sally checked quickly. It appeared that there were four or five couples who did not raise a hand, including the

Gordons. She wondered whether they were just reluctant to share intimate facts, or could they possibly not really be married after all?

"All right. We will carry on from there." He took a deep breath, swept his eyes around the room and then plunged on. "Tonight we're going to be very down-to-earth about our problem. I have invited a couple from the Foothill Theatre Company to show us what parenting is all about. They will tell their story in their own way, and then we will talk. Voila!"

With that abrupt conclusion Professor Martin stepped to the back of the room, and in his place a young man and woman came from opposite sides. The woman was costumed to represent a child, with a white bonnet over her head and ribbons tied under her chin. She was sucking her thumb. The man appeared to be her father with a hat on his head and briefcase under his arm. He was the first to speak and his voice was stern.

"Now Annie, I'm going to be gone for an hour. While I'm away I want you to behave yourself."

Annie briefly pulled her thumb out of her mouth and whined, "I want to go with you."

"You can't go with me. I have business to do."

Again the thumb came out and Annie's bitter complaint stepped up its decibels. "But there's nothing to do anymore."

"There's plenty to do." The father's voice was definitely growing impatient. "You can play with your dolls and your building blocks. Yes, and if you run out of those things you can watch the TV."

"I don't want to be alone," Annie cried, and she began to wail.

"Stop that!" yelled her father. "You know how I hate it when you make that kind of noise!"

Annie cried louder and stamped her feet and waved her arms wildly in a tantrum that built up intensity very fast.

Suddenly Father threw his briefcase on the floor, grabbed his daughter, dragged her to a chair where he laid her across his knees and began an act of severe paddling.

As Sally watched the unfolding drama she realized it was almost a repeat of what they had seen in the Gordon home. She glanced sideways at Bill and saw his hands clenching and unclenching compulsively. He was breathing heavily in obvious approval of the act.

Suddenly the actors were on their feet again. The man held up a hand of caution to indicate that there was more to come. The woman stripped off the child bonnet and picked up a shopping bag as her only prop. The man tossed off his hat and grabbed a basketball to fumble with. The roles were now mother and son.

"All right, Johnnie. I have to go after groceries now." Her voice was gentle and patient. "Do you think you can take care of yourself for an hour?"

John was not happy with the prospect. "There's nothing to do."

"You have your ball," Mother observed. "And you can play in the sand box out back."

"But I'm bored."

"Yes. I see that you are bored."

"Can't I go with you?"

"If you come along it will take twice as long, and I have to get supper ready early, because Daddy is going out to a meeting tonight."

The mother-son drama moved to its climax as Mother finally agreed. "All right. But do you think you can be a real helper this time? When I tell you to get a box of raisins off the shelf, do you think you can do it?"

"Yes. And I promise that I won't ask for cookies that you don't want to buy."

Sally sensed Bill's growing agitation as he sat next to Mike. He let out a snort of disgust. Suddenly he left his seat and stalked out of the assembly room in a passion of anger. Irene seemed ready to jump from her seat and follow, but Sally grabbed her hand and held firm until the moment passed.

The end of the dramatic skit came swiftly with the negotiated parent-child agreement to work together. The actors turned to face the audience before applause could distract their focus of attention and asked in chorus one simple question.

"Which kind of parenting do you want?"

Mike didn't stay to take part in the discussion. There was a "wounded child" who had run away from the gathering who needed his parenting, and Sally understood his urge to follow.

Her self-appointed task was different. She stayed with a confused Irene and shared in the lively discussion with the actors, which played on all the variations of discipline, and talk about the wounded child in the abusive father. When the evening came to its conclusion she smiled as the man actor took a piece of chalk and wrote on the portable blackboard a simple summary of the shared ideas:

PARENTING ACCEPTS THE
WOUNDED CHILD IN EVERYONE

"Yes, how true," she thought. "That's what makes the difference." And then a sudden wave of awe swept over her as she watched the woman actor take the chalk from her partner and draw a box around the words. It was the calling card again.

PARENTING ACCEPTS THE
WOUNDED CHILD IN EVERYONE

The evening was finished. Sally worried about Bill and Mike. She reached an arm around Irene's waist to give her steadiness. But she rejoiced at the great ideas that had been presented during the discussion. And best of all, she felt sure, here would be opportunity for Irene to have direct contact with their mentors, if that's who they really were. They could make such a difference in her life. She led the way to where they could take their turn after others had thanked the actors.

At last as they stood side by side Sally spoke boldly to the drama couple. "Josh. Sophie. I would like to have you meet Irene Gordon."

The couple smiled noncommitally in return and reached out for a conventional handshake. But when Sally turned to complete the contact, Irene was gone. She had headed for the door to the outside world and was just vanishing out into the darkness.

The woman patted Sally's arm. "Don't worry. She feels responsible for her man. This was rather early for her beginning. You'll have a chance to get through to her husband at another time."

When Sally was alone again back home with Mike, she told about the encounter with the people she felt sure must be Sophie and Josh and then reached for the rest of the story.

"So how did you find Bill?"

"I followed him into the parking lot. He was hot!"

"But he seemed all right when we met at the car to drive home again."

"You should have heard him at the beginning. 'They're crazy! Stupid! Weak! Sissies! You let kids get away with wrapping parents around their fingers and there's no end. They'll take over!'"

"That's really sad, Mike."

"I didn't argue with him. I just suggested that we go for a walk. I put an arm around his shoulder. We went down onto the green grass of the baseball diamond and enjoyed the moonlight together."

"So you played father to him?"

"Yeah. I guess that's what I did."

"You get an 'A' for effort."

"But a 'D' for results."

"Maybe. But the final grades are not in yet."

5

Stormy Hilltop

A stormy December 31st encouraged Sally, and most all Nevada County residents, to stay home. The wind-whipped deluge of rain came with a violence that, for many, was proof that global climate change was surely happening. Reports of downed power lines and widespread blackouts forced Tad and Jeannie to cancel plans to celebrate New Year's Eve with their friends.

For Sally and Mike this was the end of the first decade of the new millenium and marked the beginning of new challenge: the teen-age of Tad and Jeannie. It was the same for their neighbor across the street: Jan. Andy still had a couple of years to go. But the message was clear. TEEN-AGE time had come with all its uncertainties.

Sally seized the moment to propose a celebration in front of the fireplace. "Why don't we make the best of this awful weather? What better time to review the past ten years?" For weeks she had been hungering for an hour to help the family come closer together. *We all have schedules that are much too busy,* she thought. *If only we could sit down and look into each other's eyes.*

Mike joined her promptly in the fireplace suggestion. "Good idea. And I have important news." Sally's pride rose for she knew his "secret."

"So you want some 'family council' time?" said Tad grumpily. It was not his favorite.

"I was going to watch a TV program about the best movies of the year," Jeannie complained.

"Also, we have some special refreshments to top off our council time," said Sally. "We'll save them for the finale of the evening."

She was about to pile on further arguments, but Mother Nature made it unnecessary. The power went out. There would be no TV. Sally groped her way to the flashlight on the mantle and drew Jeannie into the task of lighting candles. Tad with a new adventuresome spirit volunteered to stoke up the fire.

When all the arrangements were completed she was pleased to see Tad stretch out on the carpet in front of the glowing logs. Jeannie chose a cushioned footstool. With Mike beside her on the sofa in comforting nearness, Sally opened up the dialogue with a bold sweeping question she had been playing with in the back of her mind.

"Why don't you two 'threshold adults' tell us what was most important during the past decade?"

A dragging silence stretched out for several minutes. She was pushing her children into unfamiliar territory. Why should they reach back into history? The present was full to overflowing. School and friends and social exploration left very little time for the family. Sally found memories from her own adolescence rising up out of their slumber. How hard it had been to win approval from her peers. How confusing life seemed with no sure place to take hold. How her best friend had turned against her for no reason at all. Sally realized she was pushing her children to take a risk.

Finally Jeannie volunteered. "Maybe it was the dress you made for me for the eighth grade party at Thanksgiving time."

Sally went fishing for more. "Why was that big?"

"Everybody talked about it."

Sally's memory of that radiant hour came back with joy. Her girl's life had been granted a peak experience.

There was another stretch of awkward silence before Tad spoke with deepest seriousness. "When Dad came home from Eureka. That was the most important of all."

"Thanks, pal," said Mike. "I would add on to that my gratitude that your mother got her wonderful job and made it possible for me to go back to school."

Sally squeezed her husband's hand with approval, but then Mike pressed on with words that brought her a strange uneasiness.

"And she has climbed very high on the capitalist ladder.

She is now one of the key managers for Venture Dress Company. And with her promotion she now owns a chunk of stock. Your mother's a genius in the world of business."

His boasting bordered on the cynical even though she knew that he was truly grateful. Tad and Jeannie did a youthful clapping of hands and a grandstand cheer.

"Yea, Mom!"

Sally found quiet wonder in the moment. The family had often exulted over her success. They understood fully how her swiftly increasing income had made it possible to pay off the mortgage on their home. But Mike's hidden feelings told another story.

Tad pursued the lead. "Is Venture your high point for the decade, Mom?"

Sally retreated into silence for a moment and finally answered with a firm, "No."

"What can be more important than having a good job?" said Jeannie.

"A good job is the result of some other things," she said quietly. "Most important, above everything else, is our contact with Josh and Sophie."

Tad sat upright in front of the hearth with new alertness. "They were great people. But I never understood where they came from."

Mike laughed. "Nor do we."

Sally smiled privately. *How can we possibly explain the mystery of the mentors? To the children, or to anyone else?* Strangely and wonderfully Josh and Sophie had repeatedly crept into her consciousness and taken hold of her deepest thoughts and feelings. They were the ones who had saved their marriage, and done much more.

Mike had shared with her similar experiences, telling how all through college studies and in his thesis work they had been there with nudges that steered him into creative, innovative designs and new patterns for research.

Jeannie protested her father's denial. "But they have to be from somewhere! Don't they?"

"Maybe," said Sally. "Maybe not. All we are sure of is that when we need them they are 'there', which I suppose means 'here.'"

"We have used their phone number. Many times," said Mike. "I'm sure we wouldn't be sitting here tonight as a family if we hadn't been able to ask for their help whenever we had a problem."

It was Jeannie's turn to sit up straighter. "You have been phoning them?" There was a light of wonder in her eyes.

"Actually quite often. Maybe once a month—or so."

Jeannie's eagerness blossomed. "Could I call them?"

"I don't know," said Mike. He turned to Sally for support. This was a new frontier.

She responded to Jeannie. "Why would you want to call?"

"Oh, it would be fun. They're such cool people."

Privately Sally mused. *That's hardly the best motive.* She squeezed Mike's hand again with a message, *You take it from here.* She wasn't at all sure which way to turn.

He smiled at his daughter. "You can try if you want. Here's their number."

Jeannie hesitated, with excitement and caution twitching her body, and then she moved swiftly to the drawing board in the shadowed corner of the living room and picked up the cell phone. She returned to her footstool and punched in the numbers.

Suddenly a deep puzzlement took possession of her. Then a frown spread across her forehead. Abruptly she rose to her feet, placed the silent phone on the fireplace mantle and stood nervously watching the glowing logs.

Sally asked softly. "Didn't they answer?"

"Recorded message," was Jeannie's short answer.

When it became clear there would be no volunteering of more information, Sally pressed firmly. "So what did the recording say?"

"Humph," was Jeannie's further reaction. "They told me I could leave a message." Reluctantly she added, "They said that when I had a serious problem they would be happy to talk with me."

"Oh?" Sally's adult wisdom moved quietly to the forefront. “That sounds exactly like Sophie and Josh.”

Jeannie returned to the footstool. “Aw, forget it. Can we get on with the family council?”

Mike moved into the gap. “I feel it’s time now to tell you about the big breakthrough that has come to me for the benefit of the whole family. This is my high point for the decade.”

Sally couldn’t resist intruding with her comment for the sake of the children. “This is really a terrific opportunity. Wait till you hear.”

But the beginning of Mike’s story was delayed. The violence of the storm increased with howling wind that pounded against the windows of the living room. It drove the family into stunned silence, until Tad, with real worry in his voice, pressed for scientific information.

“Dad, could we have a cyclone? In the foothills?”

“Not likely. Our elevation discourages that kind of pattern.”

“But with climate change happening everywhere...?”

“Right. We have to say anything can happen. Like, this season the snow pack in the high Sierras is 40 percent below normal but rainfall is 50 percent above, and we’re not even half way through winter. That means there will be very poor runoff in the summer when we really need it.”

Tad relaxed a bit, and Mike took the next step to get on with his story. “You all have heard how with the fall semester, Sierra College finally turned into a four year school. Well, the big news is that now I have a job as professor of Environmental Studies.”

“Wow!” cried Tad. “That’s the greatest!”

“I’m sure you realize,” said Sally, “that this never would have happened if it hadn’t been for Daddy’s lonely nights and hours away from us grinding out his Ph.D thesis about ‘Global Climate Change.’ He is now looked up to as one of the authorities in the field.”

Mike added, “And if it hadn’t been for Internet and my heavy commuting to Sacramento’s University, I never would have made it. But the climax came yesterday. I signed the contract. I’m to begin with the new semester.”

He turned to Sally with a smile that she instantly sensed called for guardedness. “And that can mean Mom won’t have to work at a job anymore.” And then he added gently, “That is, if she doesn’t want to.”

Sally ignored her husband’s pointed hint. “And that brings us to the next subject for our family council. Yesterday Irene Gordon bent my ear with a problem that is keeping her awake at night. Her daughter Jan began menstruating several months ago, and...”

“She did?” cried Jeannie with big protest. “She didn’t tell me. And we tell everything!”

“I’m not surprised she kept her secret. She found it scary,” said Sally.

Tad broke into their exchange. “Hey, will someone please tell me what’s going on?”

Jeannie ignored him and drove ahead. “That means she beat me in the race. What’s the matter with me that I’m so late? A lot of girls have started already at 12 and 13!”

“There is nothing wrong with you, beloved,” said Sally. “Women’s bodies are all different. Your time will come.”

She checked briefly on Tad’s puzzled face and decided to drive ahead. “Hear the rest of the story, for maybe there is something we can do to help the Gordon household.”

She was pleased to have Mike wrap a supportive arm around her shoulder, as he often did when he felt a growing tension in her mood. He was already informed of her present concern. He knew her worries over the problems of the folks across the street. They seemed to be hitting her from every part of their lives.

“Irene came to me with her news and with a terrible fear that Jan is in real danger of getting pregnant. I don’t think you two realize how awful this prospect can be for her. You see, Irene herself got pregnant when she was fourteen, and she believes it has ruined her life.”

Jeannie was plainly disturbed. “How can she be ‘ruined’? Doesn’t she have Jan to show for her pain?”

“You speak like a wise old woman,” said Sally.

“Well, why not? We have lots of sex-ed classes at

school."

"That brings me right to the point," Sally continued. "For Irene, what the school teaches is not enough. She wants something more, and she thinks that our family can help."

"What do you mean?" Tad asked, his puzzlement rising. "How can *we* say anything more than the school?"

"Oh, there's a lot more that the school doesn't touch." Sally became emphatic. "What Irene fears is that it's already too late. What I'm asking you is whether you will be willing for all of us to meet with Jan, and maybe even her brother Andy."

Tad and Jeannie stared at each other in a confusion of doubt and deep reluctance.

"The point is simple," Sally continued. "When teen- age comes along it brings with it the driving temptation to experiment. And playing around can lead to hellish stuff."

"How about we ask another question?" said Mike, picking up quickly on the challenge. "Do you two have friends who might profit from a 'graduate course' in sex-ed? If you do, we might expand this to a class, and arrange to meet in a public facility."

Sally's silent first reaction was, Whoa! *You're running awfully fast into unknown territory. Irene is asking help for Jan.* She stared at Mike. He was always ready to pioneer in unfamiliar territory. That was his forte. She watched the faces of Tad and Jeannie as they struggled to keep afloat in the deep waters, and finally she offered a conclusion. "Is it okay to take your silence as an agreement to do whatever we can to help our neighbors?"

There was no protest so she turned to Mike. "And what will Bill say to all this? Will he cooperate?"

"I doubt that he will. Hasn't Irene talked with him about the problem?"

"They don't talk about anything."

"Don't talk?" cried Tad. "We talk about everything."

Jeannie spoke softly. "Jan crabs all the time that she has nobody but me."

Mike was silent for a moment and then added his

reflection. "Of course, Bill has been in New York, off and on, a great deal during the past months. He told me he will be heading back during the first week of the new year. So, maybe he won't even hear about this problem."

"He's too busy making millions," said Sally.

"Correction," Mike groaned, shaking his head. "He's on the way to billions! It's very sure he's one of the top men on Wall Street today." And then he added what Sally again felt had a cynical touch. "He's the other successful capitalist on Lidster Avenue."

Once more she chose to ignore the veiled hint. She pushed on with their schedule for the evening. "I think it's time to introduce our Japanese fizzy drink. And you will love the New Zealand mango sweet dish I made."

"Wait a minute!" cried Jeannie. "I've got to live with Jan day after day. Do you want me to keep silent about your big deal? Or do you want me to argue her to come along?"

Sally raised her eyebrows toward Mike to encourage his answer, and to herself she smiled over Jeannie's sensitive thinking. *There's another one of my "beloved strangers."*

Mike's answer to Jeannie was gentle. "Why don't you hold off on Jan for a while and see whether any of your friends want the class."

When Sally and Mike at last were making ready for slumber in the privacy of their bedroom, the cell phone rang. It was their mentors and they both got on the line to hear what new thing might be looming on the horizon.

"You two are standing on a threshold," said Sophie.

"What lies ahead," Josh added, "is an opportunity to deepen your marriage relationship."

"But we're doing just fine," said Mike. "Our big push to get me into a teaching career is completed. The path ahead is smoothing out."

"There's a good bit of illusion in that conclusion," said Sophie. "We still have big work for you to do."

"I think I know what you mean," said Sally. "Mike and I have very different styles in dealing with life's problems.

He's male. I'm female. We often disagree."

"That's normal. That's good," said Sophie. "But what you both need is to harness those two horses so that you can pull the new loads that we are about to pile into your wagon."

Josh thrust in with a different metaphor. "What we want to do is put wings on your relationship."

"Can you give us more of a clue?" said Mike. "I mean what sort of things should we watch for?"

Sophie spoke strongly. "This graduate course you have imagined, Mike, is something new. Almost nobody else is experimenting on this frontier. Keep your ears and your heart open and we'll help you along inch by inch."

With that the phones went silent and both parents slipped in between the cold sheets of their bed. Sally's uneasiness about Mike's cynical remarks came back to haunt her and keep her from sleep. At last she ventured a gentle challenge. "Mike, honey, what were you trying to say when you connected me with Bill, calling me a capitalist?" He failed to answer. All she could hear was his usual snore.

New Year's Day brought a slackening of the wild weather with 70-mile-an-hour winds dropping toward a normal range and broken clouds withholding their downpour. At mid-morning Sally answered a ring of the doorbell and found Bill Gordon in raincoat and cap. His mood was darker than she had ever seen before. His hands were gripping each other nervously as she had seen a number of times in the recent past. He tried to look past her into the shadowed living room. His words were harsh and demanding.

"Is Mike in?"

She knew better than to engage him in talk. "Sure, Bill. Come in. I'll get him."

"No. I'll wait here."

As she walked toward the back of the house the picture of a dejected and angry Bill made her once again wish for a breakthrough in the barrier he had built against her.

Sally sent Mike back to the front room and overheard only the briefest interchange.

"What's up?" said Mike.

"Got time to talk?"

"Sure. Come on in."

"No. Better we go for a walk."

"Okay. Let me get my slicker." And that was all she heard. They were gone, heading east along Lidster Avenue.

Not until noon did Mike return, and his face was a scene of awe and puzzlement such as she had rarely seen before. He reached out to hold her hand and led the way to their sofa.

"What happened?" she asked, groping for an opening.

"You know how we've been trying for years to help the Gordons."

"And getting practically nowhere with Bill," she added.

"I know he thinks of me as friend, but today told me more about him than I ever dreamed." Mike fell into silence until Sally nudged him.

"Like what?"

"We started out toward the Litton Trail, but it was blocked with fallen trees. We turned up Hughes and then Bill began cursing. 'Damn it, Mike, you know how I never got along with my father!' I had to agree. He had made it very clear many times."

"'This time it's like a stab in the back.' That's the way he told it. And then he explained how every New Year's morning he would call his dad in San Francisco to wish him a happy New Year, even though they never talk during the rest of the year."

"That's so sad," said Sally with a growing sense of darkness and foreboding.

"Today Bill called and all he got was a recorded message. Then he checked his E-mail. All it said was, 'Call my broker.' He called. It was the first time he'd ever talked to the guy. Immediately all hell broke loose. The broker blasted Bill for all kinds of stuff he'd never heard of before."

"Like using part of their house payment to get into the stock market?" Sally questioned from familiar history.

"Yeah. He hit him with that too. And then the broker finally caught on. 'You haven't heard? Your father committed suicide. Two days ago. Poison.'"

"Oh! How horrible!" cried Sally. The pain that seized her heart was harsher than any she could remember.

"That's when Bill got in real deep. He yelled at me. 'He did it to punish me! I know he did!' I tried to get into the act, tried to be his counselor."

"What did you say, Mike?"

"I told him life and death are not that simple. I made a big point that he hadn't been near his father to know what else has been happening in his life. But Bill wasn't about to listen to me. His final word was savage.

'I know what he thinks of me!' he said. 'He thinks I'm a pile of shit!'"

Sally squeezed Mike's hand in sympathy over the impossible task of delivering help to their friend.

Mike continued softly. "Everything else Bill had to say was almost anti-climactic, because it seemed so obvious to him that his father hated him. The broker told him that he thought his father's will cut him off completely. That he had created a multi-million dollar endowment 'for some stupid environmental group,' like the Sierra Club. That was Bill's word, 'stupid.'"

Sally groaned at the stabbing judgment and added what was little more than a footnote. "Bill has always been cynical about <u>your</u> environmental work."

"How well I know. We're poles apart. But that's only the beginning. Sooner or later I'm going to...." He trailed off into silence, and Sally decided not to dig further. To herself she finished his thought, *...sooner or later I'll get to him.*

The end of the Christmas vacation brought the young folks back to their schools: Tad to Nevada Union High, and Jeannie, along with Jan, to Lyman Gilmore School. They reported to their parents how, without leaking to Jan, they had sounded out close friends about the 'graduate course' in sex-ed and had found several who thought they might be interested.

Sally accepted skeptically the news from her young people that maybe a half dozen classmates wanted to attend. Mike declared that was enough to justify a public meeting locale. At suppertime he shared his findings with the family.

"We've got a slot for the last Saturday morning of January at the L.O.V.E. Building in the Park."

Tad did a comic bit in responding. "Now there's the sweetest romance of the century! We meet in LOVE to discuss SEX. By the way, Dad, do you know where the name came from? Was there a Mr. Love who built the place?"

"No, not that. It was a project of the local Lions Club. Lions Organized for Volunteer Effort. L.O.V.E."

"It will be a very appropriate place for the group to meet," Sally observed.

"How about I put an invitation on the Internet?" said Tad. "See if we get any takers."

Sally was pleased with Tad's apparent enthusiasm. Maybe he was finding the idea of "sex" exciting. Or was he maybe just being dutiful? Privately she shared her anxiety with Mike that the project could turn into something too complicated to handle.

"Do you know what I think, my sweetheart?" he said as they retreated to their bedroom. "I think maybe we should turn this over to Sophie and Josh. There's so much to be delivered and we're...."

"Yes, we're babes in the woods. I agree. Do you want me to put in a call?"

With cell phones in hand the connection was made, and both mentors came on line.

"It's been a while since we talked," said Josh.

Sophie spoke gently. "What's the problem tonight?"

"We've taken on a tough project," said Mike.

"Sex-ed for teens?" said Josh.

"Yes. And the assignment gets bigger every day."

Sally entered the dialogue. "The truth is we've begun to think we should turn the program over to you two. When I think back to our efforts at the class in parenting, I doubt that we made much of an impact at all in helping the Gordons."

"Now don't apologize," said Sophie. "You did the best you could. It was a good start. This time you're dealing with young people who are not yet totally caught in the traps that life has set for them."

"But please, won't you take over and make it a really good thing? A genuine 'graduate course,'" said Sally.

"As you know we're always available," said Josh, "but this time you need to venture out onto the frontier of your experience. This will be an excellent opportunity to make a bold leap forward."

Sophie added a new touch. "For starters, Mike, why don't you dig out of your wallet one of your own calling cards," said Sophie. As he fumbled to obey she continued. "You can write on the back side our cue to you as you get into the class experience. Here it is."

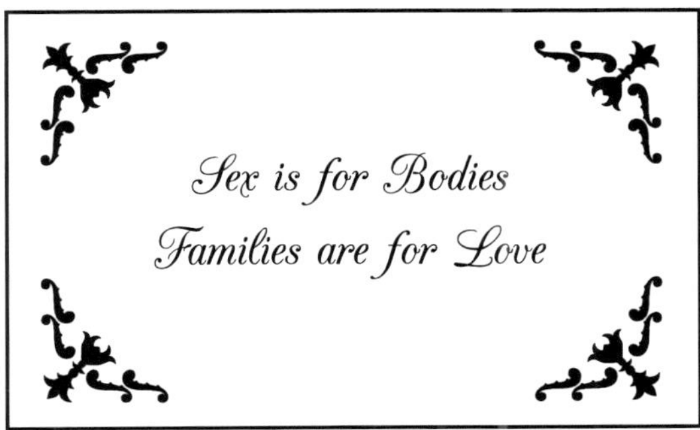

Dutifully Mike wrote the message

"And be assured," said Josh, "we'll be close at hand."

The phones went silent. Sally muttered to her mate a growing puzzlement. "What in the world can they possibly be trying to tell us?"

Mike nodded with a grim smile. "I haven't the faintest idea. I guess we'll just have to give it our best."

"But who should serve as chairperson?" said Sally.

"Do you want to take a shot at introducing the idea?"

"No way. You dreamed up the class. I'm perfectly willing for you to start."

"All right. But let's be very clear. We're both in this together. All the way. The least we can do is to share our family history with them. Okay?"

"Okay."

The Love Building

The last Saturday of January dawned cold and cloudy with a forecast of snow by evening. Mike drove the family to the LOVE Building in Condon Park, with Jan reluctantly accompanying. They arrived at nine-thirty, a half-hour early and were met by the custodian.

He appeared to Sally to be a rough workman in overalls and a heavy parka. With his help they set up a circle of folding chairs, guessing that 20 might show up. In fact he seemed more than helpful. He was definitely solicitous of their welfare, asking several times if there was anything else they needed. He was even willing to offer the services of a cleaning woman who was busy in the kitchen. Sally thanked him. And then they waited.

She encouraged the family to find places to sit, and began to watch her husband's growing restlessness. She wondered what kind of outline he had dreamed up for the class. He always pushed boldly into the role of frontiersman. That was his way. He loved to explore new territory, but this world of sex-ed could be loaded with land mines and deep pits. There was so much more the kids needed.

She felt a mother's sadness that the generation of which her children were a part seemed so much adrift. But then, the past 100 years had been hard on young people. She observed Mike pacing the room and mused at the irony of a rough logger, now an honored professor, leading a group of teen-agers in a quest for sex wisdom. What could come of it? The whole enterprise seemed really far out.

It was sweet to watch Jeannie and Tad welcome their classmates as they came in out of the thin cover of snow. By ten minutes after the hour Mike, winning her agreement, decided to begin with a total of only 12 friends in attendance.

"This morning we want all of you to wade in with both

feet as we discuss some of the bigger questions about our human sexuality. We understand that many of you have had several semesters at school. What each one of you feels and thinks about sex is important. So let's begin with each one telling his or her name and grade in school, and whether you have had one or more of the sex-ed courses the schools provide. Let's be very open with each other. I'm Mike and this is my wife Sally. We'll share the honors of providing leadership."

The young people accepted Mike's suggestions and routinely announced their names around the circle. They were all eighth and ninth graders. They all had done more than one sex-ed course. Jan was sitting directly across from the leaders with Jeannie beside her.

Sally was quietly pleased that all of the girls found the room warm enough to shuck off their cold-weather outer jackets and to reveal more of their young bodies, which were so beautiful. Two of them were wearing Venture skirts. She held her breath as Mike took the next step.

"All right, let's jump in with an important piece of history. The pill. It became popular back in the nineteen-sixties. There have been other versions in the years that followed. Since the sixties American culture has said, 'Now you are free to have sex anytime you want.' Is that what you have heard?" After allowing a moment for the class to exchange amused glances, Mike smiled broadly. "I see nobody disagrees. So everybody has climbed on the 'marry-go-round.'"

Sally wrinkled her nose at his casual introducing of their special language. She sensed it was time for her to get into the act.

"But now can you tell what the results of this change have been? Like, for one thing, it's easier to have 'fun,' sooner. And what else?"

The group was silent until one boy ventured, "What do you mean, 'what else'?"

"Like how has the new sex changed marriage and family life?"

One of the older girls spoke up dutifully. "I read somewhere that fifty percent of marriages now break up in divorce."

A boy put in with another fact. "And a lot of couples don't even bother with marriage at all. They just have a relationship."

Sally watched Jan across the circle. The way she sat in her chair, twisted to one side and face staring at the floor, telegraphed a message. Was it that she desperately wanted to retreat from this gathering of peers? Or was something harsh hitting close to home? And what was the custodian doing, hovering close in the background behind where Jan was sitting? He had shucked off his parka and seemed to be following the discussion closely.

Mike supplied additional statistics. "One figure that I read a while back says that 20 percent of families—or perhaps I should say 'households'—20 percent are single mothers with one or more children, and most of them are in serious poverty. What do you say to that?"

Several voices around the circle muttered their protest about the bad trip of young mothers having to go it alone. At that moment the door of the assembly hall creaked open, and three latecomers slipped in to join the group.

Mike welcomed them and explained, "We were just talking about households with single mothers in poverty. So now what I would like to ask everyone is, 'How can we stop the flood of broken families?'"

At that moment the cleaning woman came from the kitchen and joined the custodian where he stood behind Jan's chair. She whispered some message into his ear, to which he nodded vigorously, and then she stayed on as another eavesdropper.

Deep in her heart as Sally watched Jan she found a growing compassion for the wounded girl. There was no doubt that her father's violence was the cause. But then there was the abuse Bill's father had piled on him. That also cried out for healing.

"How about making it harder to get a divorce?" said one of the newcomers, jumping quickly into the discussion.

"That wouldn't do any good," came a voice from the

opposite side of the circle. "People just wouldn't get married at all."

Sally tried a new tack. "Can it be that we need to change our idea of what marriage and family is all about?" She wanted to underline what Mike had hinted at. "Maybe we're stuck on a 'marry-go-round'— spelled 'marry.' The real point of the 'marry-go-round' is that it doesn't get anywhere. It just spins around. We have to help America get off and get on with the real business of family."

As she spilled out her words she realized that throughout the growing dialogue, both Tad and Jeannie had been totally silent. She wondered what they were feeling.

The circle fell into silence. Was her challenge dead on arrival? Tad spoke for the first time, winsomely and proudly. "Why don't you tell them how you did it, Dad?"

Sally and Mike turned to search each other's faces. Their unspoken question was, *Can we possibly do it? Should we?* Their vote was unanimous.

"Well," said Mike, "for starters, ten years ago Sally and I almost didn't make it. We were right on the brink of divorce."

Sally picked up on Mike's introduction. "The big trouble was that we had failed to appreciate that our personalities were polar opposites. I was a talker. He wanted to take action. I needed to figure out all the angles. Mike wanted to produce swift results. I'm sure today that's the way it is with every couple, with every relationship. Each one of us represents something unique, something different. And sometimes that can be very irritating to the other person."

Mike laid a hand on her arm. "My turn again. I was out of work. Sally was on my back. And finally I couldn't stand it anymore. We had a separation instead of a divorce, for over a year. And that's when we began to see new ways. We learned that the purpose of marriage is to create family, and that family first and foremost is a way to serve each others needs. To work for the other's fulfillment."

"By the way," said Sally, remembering the wisdom of Josh and Sophie, "has any one of you ever checked the dictionary for the root meaning of 'family'?" There was a shaking of a few heads and she continued. "I was surprised when I learned that the Latin root 'famulus' means servant! Of course back in those centuries of the Roman Empire that would mean 'slave.' We've come a long way since then. But still in families today the point is that we are called to serve each others needs."

For a long moment there was silence and Sally decided for sure that she and Mike were boring the young people. As she groped for the next step, Jeannie plunged into the gap with a challenge. "Why don't you tell how you got help to rescue the family, Mom?"

"Thank you, beloved," said Sally with gladness that Jeannie was still interested in the role of their mentors. She swept her gaze around the circle and then reached for the best words she could find. "It's hard to tell, because there are so many ways to understand it. I think I should say Mike and I learned to listen to a very wise old couple. They were the ones who taught us how to create a new, good family out of the raw pieces of our selfish personalities. They spoke to us as our 'higher selves.'"

As she felt her way along Sally began to realize that her desire to tell the whole story of their deepening relationship with the mentors would be too much. Even Jeannie had not been ready for the truth. The best she could do for the young people was to give the broadest hints. A small introduction.

Mike tried to come to her aid. "One of the special things we learned is to see the other half of our coupleness as a 'beloved stranger.' That has meant that we no longer try to reshape our mate to be like what we would want. We accept the other as a specially wonderful unique being. A beloved stranger."

Sally again attended to the stiffened body of Jan where she sat directly across the circle, and she lifted a silent cry to Sophie and Josh. "Help us to help her in her need." Her next words directed to the group came because she felt a bigger emphasis was important.

"Sexually males and females are polar opposites who

are shaped by the Creator so that they cannot survive apart from each other. Have you ever heard the Greek myth, that in the beginning there was only one human being, and that the gods cut that creature apart to make the two forms of the human race? We're deeply connected."

"I'm glad you mentioned that," said Mike, "because it tries to underline the truth about the powerful attraction there is between male and female."

Sally felt a growing excitement in him. Was there some new eagerness showing in the faces of the young people?

"Really, my friends, what we need most to talk about is how to live with this drive." He left his chair and moved to the portable chalkboard. "The big thing is that the purpose of sex is to create a new person. Notice I didn't just say 'baby.' Sex is for bodies! New bodies!" He paused to let the words sink in. "So now what are the ways we have to prevent bringing a person to birth too soon? Tell me and I'll write them."

The first voice, with a snicker, proposed, "The pill."

Another called out with a touch of boredom, "Condom."

"Diaphragm," was the next voice.

"Sterilize."

Finally one of the girls protested, "I say the best way is to wait till you're married before you have sex."

A heavy silence followed until another girl raised the question, "And what do you do if you do get pregnant?"

Several voices pitched in. "Get married." "Adopt out." "Get an abortion."

Sally's attention was drawn sharply to Jan, for with the word 'abortion' she sat up straight in her chair and keenly began to watch the development of the discussion.

"So what do you think about abortion?" Sally asked the group. There was division: some for, some against.

"Let me ask a series of questions," Sally continued. "Would you consider killing one of your classmates?"

There was obvious confusion around the circle, but a common shaking of heads. "Of course not."

"When that same person was a toddler, would you kill?"

Again a unanimous negative.

"How about when the baby was just coming out of the womb? Or when the fetus was four months along? Or when the embryo was two months old?"

There was an uneasy silence.

"My point is," Sally continued, "that a person comes into existence at the moment when sperm and egg unite. The genes are in place!"

One of the girls complained. "But what if there has been a rape, or the girl's life is in danger?"

"Certainly there are times when abortion is the best choice. A mother's life comes first. But mostly ending the life of an embryo should come at the bottom of the list."

Sally's eyes were focused on Jan's face, and she saw a flush spread up into her hairline. This had to be the coded message she was waiting for.

Mike returned from the chalkboard, and there was a new intensity in his words, a groping for some way to get through the walls of resistance that were so plain among the class.

"What I want to say to all of you I also say to myself. When we play around with sex we are playing around with the possible life of a new person. I feel very sure that none of you want to do that. So what I'm asking is, 'Why does anyone play around?'"

One of Tad's boy friends answered with blunt honesty. "A lot of guys want fun."

"Some kids play around because they're bored."

Another said, "There's nothing else to do."

Silently Sally murmured to herself, *And the girls will find themselves rejected by the boys if they refuse to hang out.*

Another voice confessed. "Because we're lonesome."

Sally picked up on the image. "Lonesome. And isn't that sad! Because the truth is we're all connected. Deeply connected. The notion that we are separate is an illusion. Our bodies have the same genetic origin. Our history is our shared memory of all the things we have done together, both good and bad. We don't need to be lonely."

In the midst of her pitch to the class she had begun to

watch Mike as he stood in the middle of the circle. At first he seemed to be in deep meditation, and then his hand groped into his hip pocket and pulled out his wallet. He fumbled for a moment with one of the calling cards he always kept close, and then the wallet went back into his pocket.

Suddenly he changed his tone, almost to that of an evangelist. “What I want for all of you is to get hold of the Big Picture.” He paused to group his thoughts and Alan, one of Tad’s friends, protested.

“What do you mean by the ‘big picture’?”

“All right,” said Mike, “how long did it take to produce your body?”

“Nine months.”

“Is that agreeable to all of you?” said Mike. “On average. Some more, some less. That’s what sex is for. To produce bodies. Well, there is another answer that’s equally important.” He walked to the center of the circle and faced his questioner. “Science is clear, Alan, that it took 12 billion years to produce your body. That’s part of what I mean when I talk about the Big Picture. And the same goes for planet Earth. It’s been 12 billion years since the Original Fireball got things started!”

As Sally watched she saw her husband’s deep passion for planet Earth come rushing to the forefront. She saw him struggling to capture the imagination of this rising generation of new human beings!

“All right! But now comes the harsh question. How long did it take for humankind to bring Earth’s eco-system to the brink of disaster? 100 years!”

Suddenly Sally felt a warning signal flash before her mind’s eye. She swept her gaze around the circle to check reactions. What she saw was that Mike’s enthusiasm had become a contagion. He was talking his own frontier language and it had no connection with sex.

“What I’m saying is that humankind have pushed the destruction of the planet almost to the point of no return. I’m talking now as the new professor of Environmental Studies at Sierra College. Global warming, pollution, destruction of the rain forest, loss of the ozone layer, melting ice caps. All of these problems need people to help turn the trends around."

Sally's inmost thoughts shifted into hard protest. *No, no, no! Mike, you're getting off the track. This is a course in sex-ed. We're here to help Jan. She's in trouble.*

When one of the boys thrust into a moment of Mike's pause, saying, "What's all that got to do with sex?" she was ready to clap her hands.

Mike hesitated only for an instant and then plunged. "From one point of view, nothing. Nothing at all. But then, if you stay with the Big Picture, we can also say, everything. What I mean is our sex drive is an amazing power. It can wreck our lives. Or, through marriage and family we can funnel the desire and drive of sex into the creation of a new world!"

Oh my God! He's gone off the road into the ditch, Sally thought to herself, but as she watched it appeared that a new strange spirit of longing had taken possession of the people in the circle.

"I'm sure all of you have watched the news lately," Mike continued. "How the trouble in the Netherlands with rising sea levels is getting worse. I think you can understand that very soon that whole land will be under water."

"And the same thing is going to happen to New Orleans, isn't it?" cried one of the boys rising from his seat almost as a cheer leader.

"Right!" said Mike. Sally could see that the passion which had made him a whistle-blower a dozen years ago had taken full possession. "So now I'm going to place in your hands the biggest challenge I can imagine. Hear me clearly. It's up to your generation to save Mother Earth and with her the whole family of humanity. What you can do is to pour your sexual energies into the creation of a new kind of family, a new species of human being. The kind that will love Mother Earth and all her creatures!"

What Sally saw in her husband was an intensity beyond anything she had ever experienced before, and in the faces of the young people there was a growing awe that almost frightened her.

"And I promise that when you take hold, there will not be a moment of boredom. Nothing to do? Never again! There's a lot to do!"

He stopped. Took a deep breath and stared at his audience again.

"Sounds terrific," said one of the boys. "But where do we start?"

A girl added her puzzlement. "We hear a lot about the earth being in trouble, every day, but the job is 'way too big for us. How could we make any difference?"

Mike picked up immediately. "The change has to come one person at a time. One family at a time. It takes everybody to make the difference. I could recommend to you that for starters you could hook up with the Sierra Club or Nature Conservancy or Greenpeace. But we can do it right here in Grass Valley." He paused and flashed a glance toward Sally that said silently, I hope you will agree. All she could do was shake her head in silent protest.

Mike's eloquence reached far beyond anything she had ever heard before. "I am willing to join with you pioneering people to form a local organization to promote environmental rescue in Nevada County. And to dream about the new species beyond Homo Sapiens."

He stopped. He watched the faces of the young people, and then made his final appeal. "I know this is a big project, so I want you to take time to think it over. If you are interested you can phone me or tell Tad or Jeannie.

With that Mike adjourned the meeting. Sally groaned. *A graduate course in sex-ed spawning a new environmental movement? O my God! No, Mike, no!*

Several young people gathered around him to pursue further talk. Sally moved quietly to where Jan was standing. She took her by the hand and led away from the group to the far end of the hall.

"Jan, honey, if you want to keep secrets, that's your choice. But I'm ready to be helpful if you need me. I felt your pain when we began to talk about abortion. Do you have a problem?"

Tears were Jan's first response, and then as she stared into Sally's eyes she stepped closer and accepted a strong adult hug around her shoulder. When she finally won a measure of control she spoke in a whisper.

"I missed my period. For two months. I think I'm pregnant. I don't know what to do."

Sally answered reassuringly. "I'm glad you can trust me. We definitely do need to get help. Let's talk about first steps. Do you think we can share this with your parents?"

"Not my father. He would kill me."

Sally smiled. "No, honey. He would not go that far. He's still in New York, isn't he?"

"I think he'll be home next week."

"But can we talk with your mother about this? Isn't that an important first step?"

Jan's eyes locked onto Sally's in deepening trust. "Okay."

With an arm around her shoulder Sally led the way back to the class. When they rejoined Mike, with Tad and Jeannie, the family was ready to leave for home. They climbed into the aging Toyota. Tad's excitement with the morning's discussion bubbled over.

"Mom, it's going to happen! The kids want to start right now. And my friend Alan came up with a name. He thinks we should become the Earth Family! What do you say to that?"

"Earth Family? I guess that's on target," said Sally dutifully, for her thoughts centered intensely on Jan. "I only hope you can make it work."

"I think we have a dozen volunteers already," said Mike. "And there may be more."

Jeannie was already in the front line of the effort. "Dad, are there any special projects we could start with?"

"How about Number One, volunteering to replant some clear-cut acreage up the Yuba River?"

"In mid-winter?" Sally protested with rising irritation.

"Not that fast." Mike laughed. "Spring and summer is the time. Maybe helping Habitat for Humanity could come sooner."

When Mike pulled into the Lidster Avenue neighborhood, Sally spoke softly, "Jan and I have an assignment. Why don't the rest of you get lunch on the table?"

Hand in hand the two "women" entered the Gordon house and found Irene distracting herself with a TV talk show. She snapped it off and welcomed them with silent questions spreading across her face and her body tensed up for the worst.

Sally led the way. "What you imagined may be true. Your fears and Jan's fears are the same. I think the next step is to visit the Clinic and have the tests made."

Irene opened her arms, and Jan ran in to the long rejected territory. Sally joined them and produced a threesome hug.

She continued with questions, "What about Bill?"

Irene's voice became muffled. "He'll hate it. And if Jan needs an abortion, he'll scream. He won't allow it."

"When will he be home again?"

"Next week, I think. Saturday."

"All right. Let's go to the clinic first thing Monday morning. I'll drive you."

With deepening shyness Irene protested, "That won't be necessary, Sally. Already you've done so much for us." She was obviously embarrassed.

"No, my dear. I'll go along. It can be much more difficult than you think. And besides, you are family to us."

Irene's response was silent tears that ran down her cheeks. Sally held her in a long embrace until she could relax and let go of her tension.

At bedtime, the first moment Sally and Mike found to be alone she ran her fingers through his rough dark hair and kissed him on the end of his nose. Her anger and irritation from the time of the class had subsided.

"You really astounded me in the LOVE Building."

"I did?"

"This is the wildest dream you've ever come up with."

"What do you mean?"

"Mr. Evangelist, if you think turning the young people into environmental activists is going to change their sex drive, you're crazy."

Mike seemed to be in retreat from her onslaught. "You sound awfully sure of yourself. Why wouldn't it help them change?"

"Those boys are going to push sex on the girls same as ever."

"Hah! Do you mean the girls aren't delivering the 'come on'?"

"That's not the point. I'm just saying, there's no connection between sex and this new Earth Family."

"All right. All right! You hold your opinion. I'll hold mine. We'll see!"

Sally poked him in the ribs. "Okay. And don't try to insist on having the last word by saying that, 'ALL families are based on sex.'"

"Not on your life! That's not true!" He pulled out his wallet with a flourish. "I finally caught on to what Josh and Sophie had me write on the calling card. Sex is for bodies. That's real clear. Families are for love is something much more tricky. Didn't you see the rising spirit in those kids? They're ready to be a family. And it takes a family to keep sex under control!"

"Well, you really have been jumping through the hoops, haven't you?

"The real last word is this," Mike protested. "Josh and Sophie pulled me into this project. It's nothing I would have dreamed of myself. In the midst of our talk when I cried for more help, that's when they nudged me."

"Oh?" That was in fact her last word for the evening. Sally was stunned by his bold excited words.

She and Irene made the clinic trip on Monday, keeping Jan out of school. The tests were positive. The pregnancy was confirmed. The embryo was at least two months along.

On the way home with the two of them in the rear seat, Irene could not hold back from pressing her daughter. "Do you know who is the father of the baby?" Sally was deeply pleased with the gentleness of the questioning.

Jan kept silent with her eyes averted.

Mother pressed again, firmly. "Surely you know. And surely you know that I am with you all the way in this. Jan, I love you!"

Jan stared at her mother in wonderment. Her answer told more to Sally and Irene than they had guessed. "There were two boys."

"Two?" The shock drove Irene into silence.

Jan came forth with an answer that was so filled with anger that Sally imagined that Irene was being wounded again.

"Two different nights. They were feeding me drugs. I'll never let another boy even touch me! Ever again!"

But Irene received the news with a strength that made Sally sing praise in her heart. "All right, darling, we'll go on from there. We're in this together."

Sally shared the news with Mike at their bed time. "The Gordons are going to have a grandchild."

"Oh, no! Haven't they got enough problems to last a lifetime?"

She could see his point. The prospect only added huge new burdens to an already battered household.

In that instant the phone rang and he pulled the cell from the night stand to get on line. With his free hand he gestured for Sally to get on the other phone. It was their Mentors, with Sophie's voice coming on soft and clear.

"Good evening, folks. We felt it was time to connect with you, following your latest project."

"We're glad to hear from you," said Mike.

Josh spoke up. "Especially we wanted to say to you, 'Congratulations!' You handled the assignment remarkably well."

Sally couldn't resist. "I think we blew it. The kids didn't want any more sex-ed rammed down their throats. And Mike went completely overboard promoting his environmental agenda."

Sophie answered. "Don't be hasty. This event was only the opening of some doors. As the weeks unroll there will be new opportunities. We're all working toward the Big Picture, Sally. You need to loosen up the grip your little world has trapped you in."

"I don't get it," Sally groaned, still resisting.

"You have two frontiers for the present. Helping Jan and her family, and helping the young people learn the art of Earth Family."

Mike spoke softly. "The way I see it, you two came to our rescue. It was as though you two were right there in the room shouting, 'Family is for love,' like on that calling card. That's when I hit a new stride."

Josh's voice came clear with joyful laughter. "But we were there, right in the heart of the action. You simply were not familiar with our janitorial function, which is to clean up confused and messy thinking."

The phones went silent.

Sally stared at her husband in stunned confusion. "I still don't get it. You're promoting 'Family is for love' and our mentors are supporting you. Will you please tell me what you are driving at—-with the kids, and all the rest—-and everything?"

He smiled at her and then delivered a long kiss. "Right now I am quite sure that words won't help very much. How about we allow time for some action, some practical action? I think that will make the answer clear."

Marble Castle

For Sally the end of the first week of February brought a rising tension as she and Irene waited on Bill's flight from New York to Sacramento. The big unknown would be his response to the news of Jan's pregnancy. Sally was determined that Irene would not have to face him alone. Together they plotted that on Saturday they would be busy with a dress-fitting session in the Gordon's living room. They would begin as soon as Irene received Bill's phone call, which he always made as soon as he shuttled his little Cessna from Sacramento into the Grass Valley airport.

This would be a female affair. The focus would be on a new outfit for Jan with Jeannie standing in as advisor. Mike and Tad had already made their plans. They would be involved with a group of his school friends exploring an opportunity to do volunteer work with Habitat for Humanity.

Sally received Irene's signal at ten-fifteen. She gathered up her equipment and called out to Jeannie. "He's on the way! Let's go!"

As they crossed Lidster Avenue under cloudy skies Jeannie dug for more information, for she had become very involved with the whole plan. "Is this just an act? Or are we really going to make a real dress?"

Sally was very straightforward. "Our whole purpose is to support Irene and Jan. We have no way of knowing how Bill will take the news. I hope you will watch his reactions and tell us what you see. This is very important."

Silently in her heart Sally reached out to their mentors for guidance. *Sophie, Josh, this can be a make-or-break time. Help!*

Irene met them at her front door and spoke quickly. "He'll probably be home in fifteen minutes. I sent Andy off to play with his friends down the street. What do you want me to do?"

Sally was encouraged by the spirit of challenge that she saw in her face—-an important shift from past moods of defeat. This encounter was work for a CEO, and Sally was ready. "I think you should let me carry the ball. Bill doesn't talk to me, and I want to try to get through to him. I hope we can really find where he's coming from."

She delivered a love pat on Irene's arm and moved into the center of the room. A quick survey of the furniture that was organized for TV viewing she accepted as appropriate scenery. Jan was curled up on the sofa, gripping her knees in a tight hold that told a great deal about her tension. Her voice was full of anxiety.

"I want to get out of here. He'll kill me."

"That's not true, Jan. We've been through this before."

"I've got a friend up on San Juan Ridge that I could stay with." Her words came out as whining complaint.

"Come on, sweetie. Up on your feet." Sally laid out what she realized would mainly be her stage props. "Just remember one thing. We're all here to defend you. You're not alone."

Slowly Jan unbent her body and came to stand facing Sally, but her face and eyes were still full of fear.

"Let me drape this fabric over your shoulders and get some pins in place before your old man arrives." Sally's professional skills made the operation smooth and gentle. "And let's get a smile on your face. Relax. This is a wonderful story we're going to be telling. It's about the coming of a new person into life!"

In the privacy of her inner self she wasn't at all sure that Bill would get their message, but the game plan was laid out and she would do the best she could.

Irene drew up a chair where she could watch, and Jeannie stood by the front window as lookout. It was her word at last that brought everything into focus. "Here he comes! He's pulling into the driveway." She came back to sit as a member of the audience.

From where she was kneeling Sally flashed a quick glance as Bill strode in through the door from the garage.

She saw in his face a mix of excitement and surprise. He dropped his briefcase on a side table and stared at the scene.

"Welcome home, Bill. How was New York this trip?" Sally seized the initiative, hoping to slow down his questioning. He ignored her and demanded explanation.

"What's going on?"

Sally pushed ahead. "I promised Jan I would make her a dress in the latest fashion. This is it." She wasn't about to cave in to his aggressiveness. "But do I sense that you have some special news from the East Coast?"

The spark in his eyes confirmed her hunch. He did have something he wanted to boast about. "Yeah. And I don't mind letting the whole word hear. Yesterday I arrived at my big goal. The market swept me into the elite company of billionaires."

He swaggered his way closer to where Sally was working with Jan. "I've been shooting for this since the beginning, and now I've won!"

Sally rose up from her kneeling position and extended her arm for a handshake of congratulation. "Why, that's wonderful, Bill! That makes you one of the top capitalists in the country, doesn't it?"

She noticed that Jeannie was impressed, but neither Irene nor Jan showed any emotion. Quickly she decided that the special moment had arrived.

"And you will be glad to hear more good news, Bill." She paused to capture his full attention. "You're going to have a grandchild."

"What?" His emotion was explosive. "What are you talking about?"

Sally plunged ahead, keeping the story in her own hands. "Unfortunately the father of the baby-to-be is unknown. But Jan is doing beautifully to adjust to the situation. Delivery date will be in August. That will be time for all of us to rejoice."

"Like hell!" Bill cried. He stepped closer toward where Jan stood with pins sticking out everywhere, and Sally made sure that her own body was a wall of defense against any aggressive move.

His anger poured out. “You don’t keep secrets from me, see! Who got you into this?”

Sally kept tight hold on the action. “Bill, I already told you. The father is unknown! There were at least two boys involved. You know how things like this can happen. This is no mystery to you.”

He turned his glaring face directly toward Sally, and she could see that real confusion had taken over. How could a father, who himself in his teen years indulged in hanging out, pass judgment on his child who was doing the same?

He mumbled his excuse. “All I want to say is, it’s not a good thing.” He backed off a couple of steps, and Sally seized the moment.

“Bill! Think again! ‘Not a good thing,’ is true. But a wonderful ‘good thing’ is going to come because of this. You are going to have a grandchild! Don’t you think it’s time to tell the mother of this new child that you do love her?”

His confusion shifted into awkwardness and his anger collapsed. He turned back toward Jan to lay a hand on her head and rumple her hair. “Great, kid. Terrific news.” He spoke very softly.

It was apparent now that Bill did have strong desires for offspring to carry on his name. As one of the wealthiest men in the nation he would be looked up to with growing respect. The Gordon heritage could become very important.

Sally was determined not to lose the momentum of the hour and quickly changed the focus. She ventured into unknown territory. “So, Bill, what was it on Wall Street that pushed you over the top?”

He turned to face her and for the first time ever she felt that he was looking directly into her eyes. It was as though he was pleased that she was appreciating his unique world.

“Yeah. . That’s right. The market did it. My big holdings in oil and timber climbed high this week.”

“I can guess how you feel. I watch the way my Venture stock rises and falls. But here I am one of the little ones at the bottom of the ladder and you are at the top."

She did her best to sound fraternal with Bill even though her heart was not really deep into his specialty. Mike's cynical word about the 'two capitalists of Lidster Avenue' still haunted her. She turned back to her role as dressmaker-designer, adding more pins to the cloth draped around Jan's body.

"So, where do you go from here, Bill? What next?"

He paused just a second to send a wink of acknowledgment to Sally. His answer surprised all the women watching as he stood close to Jan.

"For quite a while I have been thinking our house is too small. Now with a new generation coming along it's more necessary than ever to expand. I'm going to build a new home!"

"Oh!" cried Sally with genuine dismay. "Does that mean you're going to move away?"

"Not very far, Sally. Last year I bought seven acres of the Litton property. Really, it's still in the neighborhood. Just around the corner on Ridge Road."

Sally's attention was pulled swiftly to Irene, for she rose up from her seat on the sofa and flashed a wordless message that told of her irritation that Bill had left her entirely out of his planning. She stalked off to the kitchen.

It was Jan's turn to be excited over her father's plans, for now she had not only escaped his harsh judgment but for the first time he seemed to be thinking of her welfare. "Daddy! Will you plan for a nursery?"

"Of course, kid. It will be a big house. Much bigger." Again he faced Sally in friendly fashion. "So now when will I get to see the new dress on the new mother?"

"Soon, Bill. Soon. This will be her maternity outfit." She added a request that had been simmering in her mind for many days. "Sometime I'd like to sit down and talk with you about Wall Street. Okay?"

"Sure. Anytime."

At suppertime she and Jeannie made their report to the men of the family, and Mike shared a puzzle that he had harbored for many months.

"I can't figure Bill Gordon and why he sticks it out here in Grass Valley. A guy whose life is in the financial world ought to live there."

Sally was ready to tell her hunch, but as she watched Jeannie's eagerness rise swiftly she chose to listen and was fascinated with her daughter's wisdom.

"Dad, I bet I know why. Whenever I see the two of you together there's a look in Mr. Gordon's face that says he's glad you're like a brother. Maybe he doesn't have any other friends like you."

"I'll vote for that," said Sally. "And now why don't you two tell us what you did today."

Tad led off with their job at Habitat. "We were painters. There were six of our kids from Earth Family. We did the whole house on the outside."

Sally pressed him with a question. "Are you really calling yourselves 'Earth Family'? I thought that was just a whim."

"No way! We've been talking a lot. We're hunting for bigger projects to heal the wounds of Mother Earth." The eagerness in his face about their enterprise gave Sally a thrill.

Mike pushed back the vegetarian plate he had disposed of and added new bits to the dialogue. "There are lots of things the kids can do. Cleaning up roadside rubbish is just one example. They can also get into waste management, collecting cans that have rebates."

Sally watched his eyes, so full of light, and rejoiced in the gladness he was finding with the young people growing out of his new job at Sierra College.

Abruptly Mike shifted direction. "I have a question; about your contact with Billionaire Bill. Did you pick up any clues about what stocks he's playing with now?"

Again his cynical tone of voice made Sally more watchful. "I don't think he's 'playing around.' He gave me the feeling that he's very much involved in directing the businesses he now owns. He said he's specializing in oil and timber."

"That's what I was afraid of," said Mike. He got up from the table and stood in lonely irritation. "That puts him in the front ranks of those who are destroying the Earth. And knowing Bill, I'm sure he's going to be grabbing for more money and 'to hell with the environment!"

His hot words burned into Sally's growing appreciation for their friend across the street. "No, Mike, that's not the way he is. He's got a gentle side, a caring side that you haven't seen."

"You're not reading the signals!" he answered sharply.

Sally could see that his emotion was disturbing both Jeannie and Tad. He drove ahead with deep intensity. "Oil and timber industries have been doing the worst damages of all. Bill is not about to insist they back off. He's a capitalist above all else; an anti-environmentalist!"

Sally slipped into silence. There were too many unknowns for her coping. She felt in her secret place of retreat within that there would have to be a deeper search for understanding somewhere in the future.

Spring came, and summer with the drought that Mike had been predicting. The thin Sierra snowfall robbed the streams and rivers of their usual flow. Fires emerged with wanton randomness, in the high country, in the Yuba canyons and even in the closely watched neighborhoods of Grass Valley and Nevada City. Smoke pollution was the most painful ever. Fire-fighting teams were pushed to exhaustion.

By August everyone had breathed more smoke-polluted atmosphere than at any other period in history, and Sally could almost hear the sigh of relief that came near mid-month when wind shift brought a week of genuine peace; the week that coincided with the County Fair. No new fires.

She and Mike were out in front of their house cleaning up around their drought-dead lawn when Bill crossed the street to make a proposal.

"Would you two be available for a picnic on Saturday? I have something I think you'll be interested in." He was bubbling with enthusiasm and friendliness.

Mike laughed. "Mystery man? Sounds interesting."

"I'll bet I know the secret," said Sally with the smile of a conspirator. "It's the new house, isn't it? Your spouse has complained about how hard and long you have been working on the plans."

"The squealer! But that's it. I think a picnic over on Ridge Road will make it real. You've got to see the dream place to enjoy it." Sally thought she had never seen him so boyish and eager.

Their foot-trek late Saturday morning also included Andy who decided at the last minute that he had nothing better to do. He'd already had enough Fair-going to last a week. Jan stayed home, for her hour of delivery was drawing near. Bill led the way, dressed in workingman's overalls, clearly one of the "costumes" he used to dramatize his various personas. He had a roll of heavy papers under his arm. Irene carried the lunch basket. Mike, at Sally's suggestion, brought a tarp.

In less than 10 minutes Bill was able to do a dramatic "Ta-da! Here we are! Here are the lots on which the Gordons are going to build their new house!" Sally sniffed to herself at his vague inclusion of Irene.

Without any doubt the gently sloping land, covered with second-growth ponderosas now more than a hundred years old, was utterly beautiful. Drying grass and scattered manzanita and dried-up sweet peas and trailing vines filled the spaces between the trees.

Dutifully Mike voiced surprise. "You are going to build a house here?"

"You bet. The best and biggest house in the county. I have more than seven acres!"

"Well now, you've got my curiosity going strong. Can you show us the dream?" said Mike.

"Sure can." He began to fuss with the papers.

Sally thought to herself, *He seems to be traveling back in spirit to his childhood. This eagerness feels like ancient dreams coming together all at once. His mood is really something new.*

"The house," said Bill, gesturing with his free hand, "will spread along the slope, half way back from the road."

Mike laid the tarp on the grass, and Bill knelt down and unrolled his floor plans for all to see. Mike joined him with a question about previous ownership. "Didn't this land originally belong to the Littons?"

"Yeah. And before them, who knows? But look. Here's what I'm planning. There will be two floors. A big living room, big enough for a convention!" He laughed. "A grand dining room with attached kitchen. Six bedrooms. Each with a separate bath. And over here at the far end, four bedrooms for the hired help."

"Wait a minute," said Mike. "I thought you said this was going to be a 'house.' You've sketched a castle!"

"Right! And that's not all." Bill continued on with an excitement that shut out all questioning and criticism. "Over here we'll have a six-car garage to take care of an RV and a speed boat on its trailer, as well as our several cars. And best of all, the whole place will be 100 percent fire-proof construction with a steel roof to shed all threat from forest fire, if one should ever come, God forbid!"

"So you're going to build with concrete blocks?" said Mike.

Bill turned to throw a look of scorn. "Hey, if you think I'm a cheapskate you're 'way off base. I'm going to import marble blocks from Italy. The walls will be two feet thick."

Andy spoke up with innocent questioning. "Is there going to be any place for a workshop? That would be cool."

"Good idea," said Bill. "I'll make space. And there will be plenty of room for a swimming pool."

As Sally watched the electric sparks fly back and forth between father and son, she realized that Bill truly rejoiced in the presence of his boy. He was ready to press on with more details of the project, but Irene, standing directly behind her husband interrupted with her opinion of the enterprise, addressing her words to Mike and Sally.

"I think the whole thing is way too big. Even half this size would be huge..."

Bill interrupted sharply with a strong protest. "Irene,

shut up! You don't know what you are talking about..."

Sally quickly intervened. "Now, Bill, stop that! Let her say what she has to say. Don't interrupt!"

He retreated, definitely surprised by her challenge.

"I only wanted to point out," Irene started again, "that even half this size would be four times bigger than we have now. I know that Bill is one of the richest men in the state, but this castle will not serve our real needs."

Sally probed, "What do you mean by 'real needs'?"

"It's so big we'll have increasing trouble finding each other. What we really need is a cozy place where we can take time to get acquainted."

Her words hung in the air, laden as they were with intense personal overtones, a passionate testimony of her deep need for a better level of understanding between husband and wife. "Bill is so busy with his castle and his world of finance that he hardly knows I exist."

Sally was jolted and thrilled by the open bluntness that was so uncharacteristic of Irene.

After an awkward pause Bill added somewhat lamely, without yielding to his mate's explosion, "Well, anyhow, this design of a house will make it possible for us to entertain the top people in my profession." He made no connection at all with Irene's world.

Sally responded with strong conviction, struggling to support Irene. "But it wouldn't be a home, Bill! The purpose of a home is to nourish family. Isn't that something you want very much?"

Mike stood up on the edge of the tarp and, with a touch of lightheartedness, he played the professional.

"Bill, I have to speak as Professor of Environmental Studies. I think you have been infected with the common American virus: affluenza. It's also called consumerism."

"Aw, get off my back," cried Bill, jumping to his feet. "If I can't enjoy my wealth now, what's the use of fighting for it?"

"Let me put the finger on just one part of your project," said Mike. "It's going to be an energy hungry castle in a time when the world urgently needs to be conserving energy and to turn back the terrible reality of global warming."

"Hey, why should I worry about that stuff?" Bill grumbled. "I'll be dead long before it has any effect on me."

In the inner sanctuary of her soul Sally shared the disappointment she felt was washing over her husband. Bill's world was the tiniest on planet Earth. Himself alone. The disease of consumerism was truly malignant, with no concern for the generations that would follow.

As she watched the standoff between the two men, a new drama came on stage. Irene took several steps directly to Mike's side and laid a hand on his arm. She looked up into his eyes and made a plea that ran heavy with longing.

"Tell him, Mike! Tell him what it takes to build a family! You're his best friend."

Sally stood in awe at the scene. Never before had Irene crossed the bridge into Mike's world. And now here she was begging for his help also. "Bill won't listen to what women have to say," Irene added. "Maybe he'll heed your man-words."

Mike stared at her, apparently baffled. He had already made his pitch. Having Irene reach into his life at close range seemed to add confusion to the moment. He patted her hand and grabbed at a straw with unfailing readiness to be lighthearted.

"Hey, we're here at the scene of new beginnings, Bill. You're the genius at gambling. How about spinning the wheel for this little lady? And anyway, isn't it about time for lunch?"

That proved to be the end of the Saturday morning excursion, for Tad, dressed in his summer briefs, came running along Ridge Road and into the midst of the gathering. "You've got to come! Jan's in labor! Jeannie is staying with her!" He was full of new excitement.

Lunchtime was abandoned immediately, and all effort was focused on getting organized for the trip to Sierra Nevada Memorial Hospital. Sally and Mike elected to stay home and let Tad and Jeannie represent the family and be the ones to pace the hospital hallways with the Gordons.

"If there's anything we can do to help, please be sure to call us," said Mike, as six of the combined families piled into the big Lincoln and took off.

In the privacy of their mid-afternoon time of watchful waiting Sally opened up unspoken concerns from the picnic encounter. "Mike, I think you were pushing Bill awfully hard."

"Well, do you think I should have gone along with his agenda?"

"No. But you aren't going to change his value system overnight."

"Maybe yes. Maybe no. What I'm really struggling for is a way to help him find healing. Without aid he's going to destroy himself and a big part of the planet."

Sally smiled and stroked his hand that rested on the sofa between them. She murmured, "I'm glad you can feel Bill's needs."

Mike burst out with new fervor. "Do you know what was on my mind the whole time we were picnicking on the Gordons' land? There's no longer any question, the rising ocean level is taking out the lowlands of Bangladesh, and millions are fleeing. Holland is gone. New Orleans is under water. And Bill and fellow Americans by the thousands are saying, 'There's nothing I can do about it."'

"You are telling the big story," Sally agreed, "that Mother Earth is solving the over-population problem in her own way."

"Not here she isn't. Not in Nevada County. Everybody wants to move out of the lowlands and come up here to build their house. To build castles! And the traffic on our narrow streets has become fiendish."

They both fell into a silence that was pregnant with yearning for a better way to manage their differences. At last Sally rose out of her resting place on the sofa and fetched the twin cell phones.

"Don't you think it's time to call our mentors?"

"Your timing is perfect, as usual," Mike chuckled. He put the phone to his ear to check the dial tone. It was silent. He waited and waited and then frowned. "Why don't you try yours."

Sally checked her cell and found it dead also. "What's the matter?"

"Let's try the main unit," said Mike and he stepped over to the drawing board in the corner of the living room. Still no dial tone. "Must be the system."

Sally moved to the front porch to check the neighborhood scene. "Mike, there are two workmen at the power pole. Maybe all the Lidster phones are dead."

He joined her on the porch, and they watched the pair. One had just climbed down the pole. With tools dangling from their belts they came up the driveway.

"Our phones are dead," Mike announced to them. "Is there some general trouble?"

"That's what we're here for," was the answer one of them gave, and then it was that Sally realized that this workman was female. Her gender was mostly concealed under rough work-clothing and a close-cropped head of hair.

"Would you like to check our phones?" Mike asked and led the way inside the house.

The woman stopped in the middle of the living room carpet with her partner close beside. "Perhaps you have been depending too much on telephone contacts."

The male workman added another strange comment which also didn't sound like a telephone professional. "Fixing technology actually is a very low priority."

Suddenly Sally found her heart leap with joy. "Josh! Sophie! It's you!"

What a perfect way for them to get past our being trapped in the busyness of everyday!

Sophie's familiar voice sang with good cheer. "We've been waiting for a contact from you."

Mike responded with his current passion. "It seems as though our problems get bigger every day. "Not just our family but the whole of planet Earth."

Josh sounded almost as though he was applauding. "And the answers are getting bigger also!"

“I’m afraid we’re not doing very well with answers for the Gordons,” Mike added.

Sophie responded. “No need for you to apologize. We’re right on the threshold of some really big developments.”

It was Sally’s turn. “Do you mean like the coming of the new grandchild?”

“That will be only an early straw-in-the-wind,” said Sophie. “The next five years will challenge your imaginations.”

“I am very clear that the next five years could be the make-or-break time for the environment.” Mike’s passion was rising again. “But what can we do, more than we have been doing, to promote healing? Don’t you have a new calling card for us?”

Josh spoke with uncommon firmness. “It’s now time for you to begin writing your own cards. Take one out of your wallet, Mike, and let Sally write on the back and get all of this into focus.” Sally received the card, reached for a ball point and was ready to take dictation, but Josh pressed harder. “No. This is the hour when you, Sally, are to formulate the necessary next step. You are fully prepared. Go for it!”

She retreated within and was not greatly surprised to find words forming in her mind. They were thoughts that had become daily more familiar. Gently she wrote her insight and Mike leaned over her shoulder to read.

Together they turned back to their mentors, but the room was empty. Clutching the card, Mike went to the front window to stare into the street in silence. Sally continued to sit quietly. She found herself slipping into deeper meditation.

These wonderful mentors have touched our lives so faithfully over the years. They rescue our marriage. They inspire our family, so that every day it grows wider. They've changed the way I think about myself. I'm not alone. They're always giving to us and loving us. I only wish there were a way I could give something back. I would love to help them nudge other people to wake up. To discover that there is more to life than being just another separate, selfish, silly so-and-so.

It was not until well after suppertime that the phone call from the hospital came with its news. Sally answered. Tad was on the line.

"It's a boy. Six and a half pounds. And Mr. Gordon insisted that he be called by the name that he chose: Bill Junior."

"Was that all right with Jan?"

"No. She cried. A lot."

County Fairgrounds

The summer after Tad finished his first year at Sierra College, with heavy emphasis on environmental studies, Sally found herself oddly outside the family circle. Mike, Tad and Jeannie all were deep into the big dreams of "Earth Family" while the center of her world was 60 miles south in Sacramento stitched to the expanding world of Venture Dress Company.

Mr. Carlson made it clear to the Board of Directors that it was her designing that had put them in the front ranks of the competition. No wonder he wanted her to be a major advisor to the Board. No wonder he had doubled her stock holdings. No wonder she needed to commute to Sacramento more than once a week. No wonder the price was a heavy estrangement.

At suppertime, which now was the only occasional time the family had to share with each other, Tad was the one at last who complained.

"Mom, we never get your input anymore. Jeannie and Dad and I would like to know what you really think about our project."

Sally had no doubts that her deepest loyalty was to the family. Her absence was taking its toll. She parried for time, with more than a tinge of guilt. In her secret place of self deep within, Sally doubted that either of her children was really aware of the philosophical tension that existed between herself and Mike. This inquiry by Tad was the sharpest tug on her conscience that had come in many months.

"Why don't you bring me up to date. Start at the beginning."

Mike protested, joking, "The beginning? Do you mean when you gave birth to Tad and Jeannie?"

"Stop that." She flashed him a smile. "Just take me back to June 15th. That's when you had the first meeting.

Wasn't it, Tad?"

"Even before that. My time in Dad's class on Environmental Studies got under my skin; the way American business is ruining the planet." Sally groaned silently. Here it is again. Mike refusing to believe that business can help to find a solution.

Tad continued. "When the semester was over I knew we had to do a lot more to wake the public up to the Earth-disaster that's getting worse every year. That's when I saw the County Fair as an opportunity."

"I confess I fanned the flames," Mike added as he reached across the corner of the table to hold her hand. For Sally it was an empty gesture. With every word the gulf was growing deeper. Environment versus Business!

Tad was exuberant. "So we agreed to get all of the kids of Earth Family together to do a brainstorming. June 15th."

"You should have been there, Mom. It was great." Jeannie burst in. "You wouldn't believe what fun it was."

Tad continued. "There were dozens of ideas tossed around, but it was Jeannie's that proved the best."

Sally was amazed by the spirit that possessed all three. "You've got me in terrifying suspense," she joked.

Jeannie filled in quickly. "What we're planning to do is build a model of planet Earth and show on the surface all the places where flooding and pollution and rainforest devastation is occurring."

"That's only the beginning," said Tad. "We're aiming for the really Big Picture."

Sally was uneasy, trying hard to go along with the tide that was flooding in from her family. "So what do you mean 'big'? Two feet in diameter? Ten? Twenty? Don't get me wrong. I think you probably have a good idea. But I'm a little afraid it could get out of hand."

Tad appeared dejected at her not jumping on board. "We won't know the answer till we try it out. Tomorrow will be our first chance. I was really hoping you would be with us."

When Sally was alone with Mike at bedtime she opened her private concern that reached well beyond the practical problems of the project. "I'm glad Bill will be in New York.

Isn't this globe going to be a declaration of war against his world?"

Mike responded with quiet musing. "Hard to predict how he'll react. So far I don't think he has a hint about the project. Both Jan and Andy have kept silence at home." He tickled her ribs. "But the important question is, are you going to be a part of the project?"

Sally grabbed his hand and kissed him swiftly. "I'll come along as much as possible. And I hope you'll lay off putting all the blame on American business. I can't help taking it personally. Also you've got to go easy on Bill. He will feel pressure from you."

"Hey, this thing belongs to Earth Family. I'm just their advisor."

"Sure, sure. But they're following your theories, Mister Professor."

"Except now theories have become fact."

"So you say," said Sally, and she snuggled closer in their bed to give him what she intended as a forgiving hug.

He responded with a grim warning. "We'll get to you, sooner or later."

Saturday morning dawned hot and dry and Sally watched out their front window as the young people gathered on the driveway. Even before breakfast Tad had moved their aging Toyota out of the garage to park in the street so as to provide a major workplace when it would be needed.

She followed Mike to the front porch to watch the work party and was pleased to see Andy and Jan with four year old Little Billy in tow. It was good that they numbered among the dozen who were present.

At nine o'clock sharp she heard Tad's strong competent voice call out, "Time to get started. Let me remind everyone again," he began with his instinctive leader role reaching out to embrace everyone present, "this is a family affair. There were ten more who wanted to come, but they were stuck with other jobs and responsibilities. So keep them in your hearts."

Sally was fascinated to hear Tad's friend, Alan, speak up. "Hey, boss, can we move into the garage? It's getting awfully hot out here."

"Next step!" Tad agreed, and the workers regrouped back inside. "Here's the plan for the day. We're going to unroll this chicken wire and cut it up into curved strips to represent 30 degrees of the Earth's circumference around the equator. I'm glad to see some of you were able to bring tin snips, as we agreed."

"But how big's the globe going to be?" Andy asked with the eagerness of a conspirator. "We've been playing around without a good answer."

"It'll be a gamble," Tad answered. "I did some sketching. Won't know till we try. So let's start with a sphere that's five feet in diameter. I think that's the best bet for now."

Privately Sally grimaced. *That's huge. It'll be a pain to hold together. Tough to transport.* But she kept her silence and watched as Tad distributed half a dozen butcher paper patterns he had prepared for the teams to use in trimming the chicken wire to size.

Suddenly the garage was too small. They had to spill out into the driveway again. The work progressed swiftly and before mid-morning the teams began the painful detailed job of twisting together the loose-end wires of the curved strips. It was physically painful for several who found their fingers bleeding where the sharp metal stabbed.

Toward noon time Sally pulled Mike back to the front porch and whispered her truth. "I've never seen them so full of excitement."

"I really think this five-footer is going to work after all," he chuckled. "I had my doubts, but look at that ball. When they get the paper mache plastered on and dried it'll be a lot stiffer."

"I'm glad to be a spectator at least," said Sally. She was appropriately awed as she continued to stare at the garage production.

Mike shook her arm to capture attention. "And now I think we should go to the kitchen and fix them some lunch. Are you coming?"

The afternoon enterprise of applying the first layer of

paper mache proved to be the sloppiest, messiest time of all. A pair of wash tubs held the water into which torn fragments of newspaper were stirred and pounded and beaten. The task drove everyone close to the brink of desperation. They found they could only make the wet stuff stick to the upper half of the wire sphere. The message was clear. They would have to let the paper pulp dry until it was firmly bonded to the wire. Then they could turn the globe upside down and do the other half.

By the following Saturday, with continuing hot weather to speed the drying process, the crude form of planet Earth stood wobbling in the center of the garage. Jeannie accepted the assignment to put tiny paper stickers around the equator to mark the longitudes. Alan led the way, with a world map in hand, to show where mountain ranges would occur. The group had a new kind of fun plastering and gluing paper mache ridges to represent the Himalayas, the Appalachians, Rockies, Sierra Nevadas, Andes and others. The job of painting on colors to represent continents and oceans would have to wait another week.

During the day of rest, with Bill still in New York, Sally encouraged Irene to come to their garage and see the progress of the Earth Family project.

She was fascinated. “What a huge world! Is this what they are going to take to the County Fair?”

“They plan to have a big tent-roof set up on the lawn outside the exhibit hall,” Sally explained. “The Earth will be sitting in the middle of a low table. And there will be a banner outside with their message:

SEE THE DAMAGE TO MOTHER EARTH.

Irene reached out to touch Sally’s arm. “You must be very proud of them.”

“And you should be proud of the way your Jan and Andy have been helping out. And even Little Billy who has learned how to stay out of the way.”

Together they made the circuit around the fragile globe and finally came to sit on the front porch. Sally switched their talk to concerns that could not be kept silent.

"When's Bill coming home?"

"Not till a week from tomorrow. I think."

"Isn't he spending more time away?"

Irene turned her face toward Sally, and she could see again the woundedness of the years. "More than a month, this time. He doesn't talk much. I think he's fighting harder. And he's angry about his castle. Been stalled for two years."

"What's the trouble this time?"

"One of the ships bringing the marble from Italy sank in an Atlantic storm. He hasn't gotten beyond the first floor. And you heard about that labor dispute in Italy, didn't you?"

"It's not surprising he's frustrated," said Sally.

"I've learned to keep out of his way. He gets irritated every time I try to make a suggestion."

At Monday supper Sally listened carefully as Mike pursued Jeannie with strong cross-questioning. "Ever since your hand got infected from that chicken-wire scratch, you have been playing around with dabbing iodine. Isn't it time you checked in with the hospital for a blood test?"

Jeannie laughed. "Join the 21st Century, Dad. I went today."

"Okay. Nobody tells me anything anymore. What was their judgment?"

Sally was concerned for his growing irritation. Was he feeling guilt for her wound? She was encouraged that Jeannie became very matter-of-fact.

"Have to wait for a couple of days while they do their testing."

Tad entered the reporting. "Why don't you tell him about the conversation you had with the technician who took your blood."

"Well, Dad, this is a scary one. I dug in with questions about germ problems. I started with AIDS and HIV wondering what more progress had been made. Then I got into some of the big world-diseases, like the epidemic in Africa. And this is what she said to me. I repeat it in her same off-handed manner. 'Hah, you ain't seen nuthin' yet'."

Mike held back for a moment and then reached deeper than Jeannie's story. "Are you saying that this professional was voicing a threat far beyond the public's knowledge?"

"Take it anyway you want," said Jeannie, grimly. "For my part I'm going to be very careful." She waved her bandaged hand. "No more chances."

Toward the end of July the Earth Family team completed their paint job on the globe. Jeannie and Tad with the help of Andy and Jan made the next step. The first black paper cutouts were pinned on the Brazilian rainforest to represent the damage done by the oil barons and the foresters.

And then Bill Gordon returned home. On a mid-week evening he crossed Lidster Avenue and punched their doorbell. Sally answered.

"Hello, stranger. You've been away far too long."

He seemed more relaxed than usual. Sally was pleased that he still appeared willing to treat her as a fellow business person.

"You know it," he answered wryly. "So long, in fact, I need to be brought up to date. What's this County Fair project all about?"

"Come on in. We should get Mike in on this story as well." Sally knew for sure that the whole truth would be very hard for any oil-man to swallow. She called her mate from the back room and made a simple suggestion. "I think it's time to show Bill the 'world'."

"Hi, Bill. Glad you're back. Come on. Let's go out to the garage." Mike punched the switch. The big door lifted up off the concrete slab and let the twilight flood in. He turned on the overhead lights and waved a hand at the globe. "There it is."

"Huh. So that's it." He circled around the circumference. "Bigger than I thought. My kids have been talking about it. So what's the point?"

Sally took in a deep breath for emotional insurance. She had fallen in love with the beautiful, colorful rough-hewn representation of Mother Earth. She nodded to her husband to take the lead.

"This is an educational project. It will show places around the planet where mankind has done the most damage to the environment."

Bill's mood changed swiftly from curiosity to challenge. "Oh, so? Like for example. What's this black patch on the Amazon?"

Mike didn't retreat. "That calls attention to the oil companies' invasion of the rainforest. The way they've built roads and done drilling and opened the way for destructive agriculture, to make worse what is already some of the poorest soil on the face of the earth."

Bill's anger smoldered. "That's a slap in the face. My people are right there in the middle, trying their damnedest to fill the world's need for oil and gas, and you are telling me to go to hell."

"Not so, Bill! I'm really just an 'advisor.'" Silently Sally corrected Mike's word to 'director,' as he continued his plea. "This project belongs to the Earth Family. The young people designed it, and they're seeing it through to the end."

Sally wanted to reach out and comfort their friend, but he was beyond help. He made a slapping gesture in the direction of South America and shouted his enmity.

"I'm sure as hell not going to let my kids have anything to do with this stupid, misguided, evil story." Without another word he stalked out of the garage into the deepening darkness and left Sally and Mike to stand alone in pain for their neighbor.

The second Wednesday of August at last brought the opening of the Nevada County Fair, and Sally and Mike joined the crowds to enjoy the biggest celebration of the year. There was no questioning in Sally's mind that this was the most beautiful park-like setting for a fair in the State of California. Tall pine trees shaded the parking lots and exhibit buildings. She found a sentimental joy in watching the merry-go-round next to the ferris wheel and the other fun trips. They all fitted right into the forest environment and into her special world of memory. “Treat Street” was the place where you could feast your hunger from dozens of menus. There was the race track with its grandstand, and out beyond were the shelters for the livestock exhibits.

As they wandered hand in hand along the paved pathway in the neighborhood of the merry-go-round Sally suddenly gripped Mike’s hand harder. “Look! There’s a clown.” Memories of a dozen years in the past came flooding in. Could this be a repeat of their encounter with Sophie and Josh at the circus in Eureka? But no. This character was different. He was fussing about, hither and yon, with a baseball bat in his hands, and he didn’t seem to care about attracting the attention of the crowds.

Mike laughed. “Not our mentors. It takes two. And this one is messing around. Nope.”

Together they moved on toward their number one destination: the Earth Family exhibit. “There it is,” Sally whispered. “Right beside the big exhibit building.”

“They did a good job on the sign,” Mike muttered. “SEE THE DAMAGE TO MOTHER EARTH.”

They stepped in under the tent roof and found the five foot globe sitting squarely on its low table, with black patches spread everywhere across the surface.

After a time of meditative silence Mike spoke up. “What do you think? Is anybody going to look in on this wounded beauty? We’re the only ones here.”

“Maybe our kids are trying to round up people to come and visit.” Sally wondered deeply what kind of dynamic could possibly awaken interest.

“More likely they’re into the fun of the Fair,” said Mike. Together they looked out at the crowd moving across the lawn and wandering into the big exhibit building. Others were headed for the amusement facilities or the grandstand of the racetrack. Nobody seemed to be attracted to the tent.

Hand in hand they wandered toward Treat Street and then their route took them into the Art Barn where local painters found plenty of spaces to exhibit their genius.

As they emerged once again into the shaded beauty of the Fairgrounds the first thing that struck their ears was the sound of police whistles. Several of them. A number of people were running across the lawn toward the large exhibit hall. Sally and Mike followed out of curiosity.

Then it was that they saw a cluster of their Earth Family young people crowded around the tent. Sally uttered a cry of dismay. “Look at the globe! It’s been smashed!” It was lying outside the tent battered and bashed into a distorted mass, with the paper mache beginning to peel off and the chicken wire sticking out here and there.

Tad and Jeannie turned to meet them along with several of their friends.

“What happened?” cried Mike as he bent down to examine the wreckage.

Jeannie had only fragmentary information. “We were just coming back from our tour of the grounds. . .”

Tad interrupted, “And I watched a clown with a baseball bat running into the exhibit hall. When I saw the wreckage I chased after him.”

“He really made a mess,” said Jeannie. “Look at it!”

Tad added more to his report. “I couldn’t find any trace of the guy. I yelled for the police to help. They are trying to find him, but haven’t come back yet.”

Mike’s anger boiled over. He hissed softly to Sally, “Stay here. I’m going to do my own searching.” He ran in through the rear door of the Exhibit Building.

Sally stepped closer to the damaged globe to see if there was anything that could be done to rescue it from total loss.

Alan who joined the cluster belatedly made a special plea. “There’s a reporter from the Union with his camera. He wants the story of what happened.”

Sally joined the young people and watched as Tad shared what information they had, and spelling out clearly the purpose of the exhibit.

The reporter pressed hard. "So what are you going to do now?"

"I'm afraid we've lost the battle," said Tad, grieving deeply. "There's no way we can repair the globe in time."

The reporter responded strongly. "I think you will make a mistake to quit now."

Jeannie broke into his speech. "You mean we should put this wreckage back on the table and . . ."

Sally caught sight of Mike returning to the tent. He was carrying a bundle of cloth in his arms.

"I found the clown's costume," he called out. "It was in the men's room stuffed into a waste can."

The Thursday morning edition of the Union featured the anguished people of Earth Family and their globe. It was in the center of the first page. The crowds came to see the wreckage. They went their ways with a vivid image of the troubles that afflicted the planet on which they were privileged to live.

Sally watched with fascination as Tad and his cohorts worked overtime in their role as interpreters to explain more of the environmental problems they were working to correct. And Mike was always close at hand as backup whenever there were bigger questions that certain visitors brought. The most common: "What's the best thing I can do to cut down on the pollution my auto spews out into the atmosphere?"

On the third day of the Fair Sally overheard Alan cheering to Mike about the exhibit. "Hey, we have a winner. A battered globe is better than a beauty."

Sally found herself serving the young people as monitor to be sure they would take time off from the intense encounters they were experiencing.

"Okay, Alan, it's your turn to run around the track..." "Okay, Jeannie, you're next. Go on over to Treat Street..." "Okay..." There was no doubt that her enforcing the rest breaks helped to bring healing to their broken world.

Late Sunday afternoon, the final day of the Fair, Tad

came back from his slow walk around the abandoned racetrack and reached for Sally's hand. "Got to talk to you, Mom."

She felt his tension as he led her out into the middle of the green grassy space beyond the globe's tent. "There's a strange look in your face. What's the matter?"

"I had a very awesome encounter. I was doing my race track walk when a couple met me face to face and wanted to talk. I'm sure they were Japanese. Their English was very clumsy."

Sally pressed him, eager to hear more. "What did they want of you?"

"They told me our exhibit was great, but that now we needed to get into big time." Tad hesitated again as though not being certain where to turn next.

"Like what, Tad? What kind of 'big time'?"

"You won't believe this. They said I should go down to the Honda agency in Sacramento and volunteer to be their agency in Grass Valley for. . ."

Sally was awed by the intense emotion that was choking her son as never before in her memory. She waited, fighting for patience, for she began to realize that something very powerful was happening in him. This was more than a casual encounter.

"The man said they were beginning to market a new kind of auto; one that was powered only by hydrogen gas and would be one hundred percent non-polluting. Mom! He wanted me to be the agent up here. He said that I should check with a Mr. Yamamoto. But I told him I didn't know anything about autos or agencies or hydrogen or business or anything like that. There's nothing farther from my experience."

"Well—-" said Sally. "I can understand your frustration."

"But then the woman said, in her broken Japanese, that they understood, but that I should—-and here's the really weird thing, more than all the rest—-she said I should get together with my Mother. That you would show me the way."

Sally stood in deepest silence. *Oh, my God, this is really a change. Our mentors are now talking directly to our children.* She finally pulled herself together and spoke softly to Tad.

"Can you tell me how you parted company from the Japanese couple?"

"Yeah. I guess I mumbled a 'thank you' some way. The man handed me their calling card. 'If you need to get in touch with us,' he said. And then they started walking again, right past me. They left me staring at the dirt race track. But in just a second I turned around to look at them again. . .and they were gone."

Sally's heart was beating harder. "Tad, will you let me see the card?"

He dug it out of his shirt pocket. She turned it over to the back side, to read a message which she expected to find.

She turned the card to its front side and found the familiar phone number.

Sally took her son's hands into her own and stared deeply into his eyes. "Tad, I'm sure you have just had a contact with Sophie and Josh. This is amazingly similar to the experiences your Dad and I have had over the years."

"But, Mom, what can I do with this? It's impossible!"

"Not really. There are two things to do. You need to keep in touch. You have their phone number and you can use it when you are facing tough decisions. The second thing—- it's what Sophie said—-your Mother'll be more than happy to work with you on this project."

A strange stabbing sensation thrust into her heart. *Does this mean my boy will leave the camp of his father and join my "capitalist world"?*

Ridge Road

The year following the County Fair brought a series of surprises to Sally that set her feet on a new path. By January she had helped Tad through the complicated business of establishing an agency to market hydrogen powered Hondas. She was amazed that by June he had toted up sales of ten non-polluting autos.

What she had not anticipated was the response of the Earth Family young people. Alan picked up the chairman job that Tad had to lay aside and launched a program to put solar panels on most of the neighborhood rooftops.

It proved to be a parallel business, for the big benefit was that the panels delivered electricity which produced the hydrogen needed to power the fuel cells of the Hondas.

Sally herself, with Mike's hearty support, was the first purchaser of the new non-fossil fuel cars. She felt that Tad's involvement in the world of business, even while he continued his environmental studies at the College, was an omen of the future. He could help to balance the growing polarity of the family.

On a Saturday morning in June, following breakfast, she sat meditatively looking out the front window at the elm tree across the street. Tad approached her with gentle persuasiveness.

"Mom, could you possibly find time in your busy schedule to do me a favor today?"

"Such as?" She smiled at his growing sense of salesmanship, but his demands had finally aroused resistance. She had her own work to do.

"I have an appointment to demonstrate the Honda, and I would like to have you come along as observer." He hesitated for a second. "And also I would like to use your car instead of mine."

"That's a switch. What's the point?" She watched him

with guarded fascination.

Tad seemed a bit embarrassed. “It’s just that my potential customer has been looking at your car, where it’s parked in the driveway, and I think that yours might make the difference.”

“A neighbor has been admiring ours? Who?”

Tad stalled while he looked out the front window and finally mumbled, “Ah, Mr. Gordon.”

“You’ve got to be kidding!” The impossibility of Bill giving a second glance at a competing hydrogen car was too much to imagine.

“He agreed to check in this morning.”

Sally found a flood of thoughts and questions racing through her mind. What could this possibly mean for a hard-liner oil man to even touch the enemy competition? Curiosity pushed her other concerns aside. A Honda for Bill? This was too big to miss.

A short time later she found herself sitting in the back seat, with Tad at the wheel and Bill beside him posing questions that were very curiously ordinary.

“So how do you get your tank filled with hydrogen?”

Tad was creative. “Several ways. Let me drive you down Hughes to the station at the corner of East Main.”

He turned the key to activate the power and the car moved in total silence along Lidster and turned onto Hughes. “This station was the first to get on board. There will be more.”

Bill kept his silence and watched as the car headed down the steep hill. Tad continued his pitch. “Right now we’re not using our fuel. The batteries are being recharged as we roll downhill. But the best thing of all is that we have equipment that will make it possible for you to fill up at home.”

“At home?” Bill was stirred by the option.

“Solar collectors mounted on the roof of your house can send you an electrical current that will break water into hydrogen and oxygen, and you can make your own fuel.”

Bill swung around in his seat with a demand for Sally. “Is that how you’ve been using the panels on your roof?

Making hydrogen?"

Sally was delighted with the open curiosity that seemed to have taken possession of him. "It's really very cheap to do it that way, Bill. I'm sure you've seen our pressure tank by the side of the house."

Tad steered the Honda into what was now a hybrid station, selling both gasoline and hydrogen. He demonstrated the simple procedure for filling up and commented casually, "This tank-full will cost about five dollars instead of twenty."

Bill was quick to respond. "But the initial investment is a lot bigger, isn't it?"

Again Tad the salesman played his skills. "True. But in the long haul it's cheaper and will continue, with increased production, to get even more economical."

Sally was fascinated that Tad carefully avoided any reference to oil and the pollution of fossil fuels. He understood exactly where Mr. Gordon was coming from—-the world of conventional thinking.

In the middle of the afternoon, while she was resting from the adventure of the morning, she encouraged Mike to join her under the sun-shade on their back lawn. "I think you would be very pleased with the way your son dealt with our oil baron across the street."

"So you're going to tell me that Bill caved in and bought a Honda?" It was the voice of the unbeliever again.

His irritating response she met in a new way. "I'm not going to tell you anything, so long as you come on with a voice that says Mr. Gordon is a hopeless capitalist like me." She poked him in the ribs and laughed at their opposition, which ever more frequently came into focus on environmental problems.

"All right," he growled. "Why don't you give it to me blow by blow, right here on my chin?" He added contritely, "After you have forgiven me."

Sally smiled, let go of the contest and continued her story. "Tad put Mr. Gordon in the driver's seat after we tanked up, and I could see he was pleased with the smooth performance of the hydrogen car. He drove up East Main and turned onto Sierra College Boulevard, right past your school. And then he took us directly to his marble castle on Ridge Road. Have you seen the progress lately?"

"Nope. And I'd rather not look at it."

Sally was sad over her husband's continued resistance to what he considered an offence to the environment. "Well, you ought to take a look. The second floor is in place. The roof's on. The swimming pool is almost finished. The place will be magnificent when it's all together. The marble walls are beautiful!"

Mike wrinkled his nose in scorn. "He's dragging it out forever. I hope he takes another ten years."

"It's possible," Sally had to agree. "Sometimes I think Bill's more interested in supervising every detail than in getting it finished."

Mike snorted. "My hunch is they'll never live in that monstrosity. Come on, let's get back to the story of the Honda salesman. Okay? So Bill told him to go jump in the pool?"

"Surprise! Tad has another believer. Bill agreed to buy!"

"No way!" The expression on Mike's face was something Sally had rarely seen. Total disbelief.

"I know what you're feeling. This doesn't add up. It would have to be the beginning of a reformation."

Mike wouldn't back off. "The truth is still the same. Mr. Bill Gordon is the CEO Ogre Oil Oligarch who along with other capitalists—-please forgive my use of the label—-is destroying the Earth in their greedy grab for bigger profits. I'm sorry, Sally, I have to speak out!"

She held her peace for longer than usual and then shared her concern. "I have to say it again. You don't see the whole picture. Bill has a gentle side. I saw it best in the way he walked us through the new house."

"Castle," Mike mumbled.

"I'll ignore that for the moment. What I saw in Bill was a little boy playing with his new toys. More than ever before, I saw him as a wounded, deprived child who at last has in his hands what has been denied to him all through life. It was charming to watch him."

"Okay," said Mike. "You keep your Bill. I'll keep mine."

In the midst of a hot spell on the Saturday following Independence Day Sally rejoiced that all four members of their family found a rare moment to have lunch together. This was catch-up time.

Jeannie interrupted her absorption with one of the egg-salad sandwiches to announce that she had decided to continue with a second year at Sierra College.

Tad's word was mixed. "Maybe sometime I'll get back for more study but right now I'm having too much fun getting Hondas into everybody's garage. Maybe I'll write a thesis on non-polluting autos and how the community loves them."

Sally rejoiced at the way Mike supported his son. "What you are doing now is far more important than what all the academics are talking about. Go for it."

Her own report hinted about developments in her work with Venture. "I don't know what to think about discussions we're having with the Board of Directors. They're talking about moving shop to El Salvador."

Tad was quick with doubts. "Hey, that's lousy. Would that mean you'd have to relocate?"

"Too early to tell. I'll keep you posted."

Mike opened up with new stories about the global environment.

"We're not making any progress," he grumbled, as he bit into a crunchy slice of apple. "In fact the planetary scene is getting worse."

"So what do you want to happen?" she pursued as she had many times before.

He ignored her question and poured out crushing details. "New deserts are forming in our richest farm lands. Starvation is on the increase in many countries, and new diseases are emerging every day. The rate of species extinction is accelerating. And our people are not acting to turn things around."

"Let me try again," said Sally. "What is it you want?"

He stared at her, as from a distance. "My students are great. They're concerned. But they're only a handful. We need a tidal wave of 'eco-caring' to wash over the nation, over the whole world."

She joined his sadness and worry for she did not have any of the needed answers either, and could not hide the fact that her world was capitalist, not environmentalist.

"I'm sorry to load my troubles on you," said Mike. "Also there's another bit of news that's not getting much attention in the daily press. Something's happening in Mongolia that has me worried. There's a new virus. They're calling it M-718. It's deadly. No cure. It appears to be spreading into China. I'm picking up scattered bits of information on the Internet."

The family sharing was broken by a rough pounding on the front door, and Sally guessed immediately that it was Bill Gordon, for he never used their door chimes to announce his presence. Mike went to answer the noise, and Sally could see Bill and feel the fury of his anger and confusion. He tried to peer past Mike into the depths of the house.

"Is Irene here?"

"No, Bill. Come on in. What's the problem?"

As Bill lunged past him, Sally noticed that he was carrying a revolver in his right hand. Bill's passion increased as he barked out his story to the group at the table.

"I got home from San Francisco half an hour ago and found nobody. I had phoned ahead to check on Irene. But now she's gone. And Jan and Bill Junior too."

Sally spoke gently. "Why don't you sit down, Bill? We can work more surely toward solving your problem."

As Mike arranged another chair Sally retreated into silent contact of love for Irene in all her pain. What she had been seeing in her neighbor and friend was a powerful growing shift of spirit. Irene the meek and obedient was being replaced by a new person, a woman who had decided she would no longer put up with abuse, a woman who was developing the courage to act to affirm her own integrity.

On the previous Friday Sally had listened to Irene pour out her woe. "For 17 years I have been obedient. He cares nothing about my needs. Yesterday he delivered one more last straw. He slapped me for telling him to quit interfering in Andy's life. I'm through."

"You say you're 'through.' What does that mean?"

"I read in the paper about the Domestic Violence Coalition. Do you know anything about it?"

Sally delivered encouragement. "It's excellent. Success record is very high."

"Well, I'm thinking that's my next step."

That was Irene's moment of decision a week ago, and now, as Sally watched Bill sag onto the new chair at the table, she rejoiced that Irene had at last acted.

Mike pursued the obvious threat in Bill's right hand. "Why the gun?"

"What gun? What are you talking about?"

It was painfully clear to Sally that Bill's pistol scarcely touched his consciousness. Carrying a gun was one of those automatic things that came with a value system totally different from what she and Mike held. She watched Tad and Jeannie absorbing all the details of the drama being acted out. Maybe this was the time, she thought, for them to confront the reality of the Gordon world, especially Bill's attachment to guns.

"Oh, this?" Bill finally acknowledged and slid the revolver onto the table. "I always aim to be prepared for anything."

Sally recalled the arsenal of weaponry that she had seen mounted on the wall of the Gordon's living room. She focused her eyes directly on Bill's and leveled with him.

"I've been listening to Irene for months. I'm quite sure you can find information about them at the office of the Domestic Violence Coalition."

"The what?" Bill shouted.

"It's the agency that helps families work through their problems. It's also known as the DVC. If a couple find themselves in violent opposition to each other, the people down there have the resources to create peace and cooperation."

Sally noticed Mike nodding his vigorous approval. She had avoided pointing a finger at the one who obviously was the aggressor. Tad and Jeannie were being especially alert as they picked up on these deep-flowing problems of family life. Their eager silence told her that they were standing in the center of one of the great classrooms of life.

Sally continued, "I think the best thing would be for Mike to drive you down to the office."

"I should get the police," was Bill's hard response. "And get the law on this case." But then he softened with a growing uncertainty. "Shouldn't I?"

"No. You will find that the DVC will help with those contacts when they are needed. Your first step will be to check in and tell them your problem. Okay?"

Mike pursued one of the fundamentals that could too easily get lost in the turmoil. "Bill, before we go you must have some lunch. You'll need all the strength you can muster. Come on, now. Here's a plate. Dig in."

Sally was glad for her husband's gesture. In strangely uncustomary fashion Bill yielded.

When Mike returned from their afternoon trip to the DVC office he saved his report to Sally for a time just before supper when Jeannie and Tad were home and could participate.

"I'm really surprised," he declared, "how thinly Bill understands about domestic violence. When the director assured him that his wife and children were fed and securely cared for in a 'safe house' his reaction was really dumb. 'Well, where are they?' he yelled. 'I want to talk with them!' He was ready to charge out in search of their hiding place. The director was very patient. "No, Mr. Gordon. Other things come first."

Sally was fascinated. "Do you suppose Bill is completely compulsive when he hits Irene? Doesn't even know he's doing it?"

"Could be."

Jeannie reached out with her special concern. "Do you know where the safe house is, Dad? Could I visit Jan?"

"I do know. But I'm sworn to secrecy. You'll have to wait. That's part of the rules of DVC."

"So what's the next step?" said Sally.

"The director talked very personally with him about the problem of spousal abuse, and how the law provided that abusers must enter a support group with other men. To work out new ways. But again his reactions were off the track. When we were alone out in the car his response was violent. 'To hell with them. I'm going to get a lawyer and fight this.'"

Sally rejoiced to watch Tad join the family's concern. "I bet he'll refuse to join the support group."

"That's what I was afraid of," said Mike. "That's why I volunteered to go with him. Maybe then he'll attend."

"Honey, that's beautiful!" said Sally. "You did the perfect thing!"

Mike shook his head. "Not as good as it sounds. I was so mad about the way he was treating Irene I was ready to launch an all-out counter attack."

"Attack? But you didn't, did you?"

"Nope. My cell phone called me to pick up the receiver. It was Josh and Sophie. They warned me that I was about to give him a spanking when what he needed was my patient, tender, loving care, no matter what. I shut up."

Mike regularly reported back to the whole family about the progress of the Men's Support Group meetings. After the third session he came with encouraging news.

"We had a modest breakthrough tonight. I decided it was up to me to set an example for Bill. I told the group that I also was an abuser."

Sally interrupted sharply. "But you never did violence against me!"

"Oh, but I did—in my own fashion," said Mike. "I blamed you for nagging at me, back in the days when we had our trial separation. Blame is a kind of violence."

Sally watched joyfully the strong fascination that had

taken possession of Jeannie and Tad. They were understanding that their father was only a "gentle abuser."

Mike pressed on. "I think my confession helped Bill to open one little door to his inner world. He told about how his father whipped him for little stuff that he didn't think was very important."

"Like what, Dad?" was Jeannie's eager reaching for more of the picture.

"He remembered one time when he was about seven years old. He failed to pick up his blocks from the middle of the living room carpet."

"He was whipped for that?"

"And he also spoke about how his mother died when he was barely ten. One day she was there and the next day she was gone. He never could get an answer out of his father as to how she died."

"Wow!" said Tad. "That's a tough one!"

"Anyway," Mike concluded, "we're on the trail together and we're making some progress."

Late in October Sally received a phone call from Mr. Carlson that disturbed her more deeply than anything she had encountered in her business career.

"Sorry you had to miss the last Board meeting," he began. "I know you had some doubts about the proposed move to El Salvador. They finally decided we had to act, with no more delays. Three members are now in the midst of setting up the new workshop."

"What about my work?" Sally demanded, knowing already what his answer would be. "Do you expect me to move to Central America?" She needed to keep the pressure on him.

"Not at all," Carlson argued. "We'll ship your stuff down there and they'll ship the finished product back to us."

Following supper, with the family gathered in the living room, Sally shared her news and her doubts. "I don't like this at all."

Tad was eager to dig deeper into the world of his business-mom. "What's wrong with El Salvador? Won't it give poor people some profitable work to do?"

"Work? Yes. Profitable? I doubt. The problem that has bothered me the most in our discussion with the Board is one thing: profit. Venture Dress wants to escape our labor laws that dictate minimum wage."

Jeannie put in her word. "You're afraid it will be sweat-shop?"

"I am. And I don't like it."

"And there's nothing you can do?" said Mike.

"I'm stuck," said Sally.

There was a moment of meditative silence, which Jeannie finally broke. "Mom? Have you talked to Sophie and Josh about this? Maybe there's a better answer."

Sally's heart warmed with tenderness over her girl's question. "You are right. The time is now."

Mike handed her a cell phone and she punched in the number.

"Hello. Sophie, here."

Sally started to speak of her concern. "I have a problem with Venture...."

Josh interrupted gently. "You have the whole family together. Why don't you use the new technology that makes it possible for others to participate?"

"New tech? But of course!" She turned to her husband. "Mike, can you turn on the TV for us? We can try out the telephone connection."

Mike snapped on the power and turned the channel selector to the program number. Immediately two smiling faces came on the screen. They were brown-skinned natives of Central America.

"Now that's better," said Sophie. "Can you all hear me?"

Jeannie clapped her hands. "How wonderful!"

Tad was speechless for the moment. For him it was a new view of the mentors. He waved his hand wildly toward the TV and finally cried out, "Can you see me?"

"Of course," said Josh. "We're all here together, even though thousands of miles apart."

"So, now, what's your problem?" said Sophie.

Sally was eager to hear their counsel. "I'm confused about Venture Dress's relocating in El Salvador. I'm afraid this will turn into an exploitation. I certainly will not go along with that sort of thing at all."

"We have a very simple suggestion for you." The two mentors turned to smile at each other for having spoken in chorus. Then Josh deferred to his mate.

Sophie spoke boldly. "Sally, sooner or later you need to pay us a visit. We'll be looking for you to come to us sometime before Christmas. Come here to the hill country of El Salvador and see for yourself exactly what's going on. Okay?"

That was the end of their conversation. The TV went blank, and Jeannie burst into ecstatic approval. "They're absolutely the most wonderful people I've ever met! They're telling us something very important."

"Like what, dear?" Sally was caught up by her daughter's excitement and the radiant light in her face. She seemed to have made a giant spiritual leap.

"They're telling us that when we're struggling with a problem we should listen to a voice that's deeper than reason."

Sally turned to Mike. "Well, there it is. How many surprises can a person absorb in one lifetime? Our girl is way out on the frontier." But she saw his mind was elsewhere.

"I'm not comfortable about your spending time in El Salvador. It's heavy with habitat decay. It's dangerous."

She smiled at his loving concern and his swift by-pass of Jeannie's vision. He had a different agenda.

As the evening shadows crept in through the windows of their living room, she mused ever more deeply over the call of their mentors and her mate's caution. *I really should go, but how can I win Mike's approval for the trip?* She knew she did not have an answer.

Mike's world included many things that were unique, and he drew the evening to a close with one of his favorites. "Anybody want to watch the sunset with me?"

Sally found comforting satisfaction that the family as a unit was happy to share with him his love of nature. He reached for her hand and they followed after Tad and Jeannie as they headed into the back yard.

The sky was filled with broken, high cirrus clouds and the sun had already dropped below the horizon. Gradually a dark red color spread from the west to the east until the entire dome of heaven was painted deep crimson.

Sally spoke softly. "I've never seen such a sky. It's awesome. Almost threatening."

Silently in her innermost heart she wondered if this were a warning omen of things to come. This new path of her children growing, of Venture Dress going off shore, of Bill and Irene's deepening crisis. These both saddened Sally and yet gave her hope.

El Salvador

It was not until the middle of November that Sally was able to soften Mike's resistance and clear her calendar so that in good conscience she could make her trip to the Central America outpost of her dress business. Her promise to phone home each week, instead of relying on E-mail had modestly helped to persuade him that it was a necessary journey.

She kept the calls brief, focused on her well-being, without getting in deep to what she was finding about the work scene, both positive and negative.

"Mike, you won't believe how wonderful these people are. They have taken me in like a sister or cousin or aunt. I'm not boarding with the management. I'm staying with the working people. They are just like family to me."

His early responses were predictable. "Hey, isn't their living real primitive?"

"Of course. But it's decent. And I love them. And Sophie and Josh are regularly close at hand to steer my education." She held back from giving details that would stir him to further questions. There would be no end.

During her second weekly call Sally shifted the focus of their talk to the Gordon household. "How are Irene and Bill getting along? And their young people?"

"Just fine," was Mike's quick answer, and to Sally it sounded too much like passing by of important news.

"Well, how about the work on the castle?"

"The castle? Hmmm, I get the feeling from words I've had with Irene that for the first time Bill is asking her advice on what kind of décor she would like. But—-" he stopped abruptly and laughed. "I'll believe it when I see it."

"Are you actually breaking your habit and paying visits to the new house?" Sally continued to reach for a solid answer.

"I'm watching. But Bill isn't making much progress yet. I'd say the place is only eighty percent finished."

Their phone call of December 15th brought a severe jolt to Sally's enterprise. Mike's voice was full of sharp anxiety.

"Sal, you've got to come home right away. The Virus M-178 has made landings both in the Pacific Northwest and in South America. Apparently jet streams from China and Australia are carrying the bug. You will be in great danger. Come! Now! And if possible get dust filter masks to wear on the planes."

Sally did cut her visit short, reluctantly, and made it back to Sacramento by the twentieth of the month. She stayed overnight with Mr. Carlson's family and arranged for a special meeting of the Board of Directors to hear her report. Two days before Christmas she was home again in Grass Valley. She made it to Lidster Avenue in time for supper which Jeannie and Tad had prepared. She truly enjoyed the familiar menu from which she had been separated for more than a month: broccoli, tofu stroganoff and apple pie. She began the family dialogue.

"What I want to hear first is some hard facts about the Virus M-178 problem."

Mike was slow in responding. "I'm not surprised you haven't been able to get the story over the Internet. Nobody seems to have any solid word. Lot's of rumor. But when I tapped into a report from Seattle that there had been a dozen deaths, I knew we were in deep trouble."

Sally watched the faces of her two children and realized that they were struggling with major worries. They kept silence and she guessed they were just "going along" with Mike's professional research. She kept on with more questioning.

"Tell me about the disease. What are the symptoms?"

"So far as we can tell the virus is carried on dust particles or water droplets. When they are inhaled they swiftly multiply in the lungs; clog all the passages; cause suffocation; takes only two or three days. You realize of course, there is a lot more they have to research."

Jeannie entered the dialogue. "I asked one of the nurses at the hospital if she thought inhaling pure oxygen could save a person's life. She didn't know. But her guess was that if there were an epidemic there wouldn't be enough O-two tanks to go around."

Tad had a question. "Dad, did you find out when the United Nations report would be announced?"

"The latest word is, soon after New Year's." He turned squarely toward Sally. "You want my hunch? I think this is Earth's method of challenging homo sapiens, who has become the most destructive species ever to breathe the atmosphere of the planet."

Sally winced. "I hate to hear you talk such stuff. Humanity is not that evil."

"I didn't say they were evil. I said they were the most destructive. They haven't wakened up yet to the hell they are creating."

The trend of their talk was producing a roadblock for Sally. She changed the direction. "All right. Do you want to hear my report about El Salvador?" Her instinct was true.

"Yeah. You've been too secret!"

"What little Spanish I could speak proved to be very useful. I talked to everybody: supervisors, workers, families, children. But I did something even more important. I used my digital camera and took action pictures of everything. I got their emotions on record."

"Can we see them?" cried Jeannie.

Tad was equally eager. "That would be cool!"

"I showed them to the Board of Directors in Sacramento and am letting them do several re-runs. After they're through, you can see them too."

"Okay. So what does your movie accomplish?" Mike was pushing hard for results.

Sally was blunt. "My visit confirmed my worst fears. If they don't accept my recommendations about doubling wages and improving working conditions, I'm going to resign."

Mike's reaction was something to behold. Across his

face she saw wonder spreading, a smile as though he felt she was coming home. Was this a sign that their capitalist-ecologist abyss was being bridged?

The holiday period slipped by swiftly with all in the family apparently enjoying their togetherness. Sally had a lot of catching up to do with each one, and also with near neighbors and especially the Gordons.

On Tuesday morning after New Year's Day she and Mike were together in an early breakfast, commenting on their observation that Bill had already gone over to the site of his new castle, when the phone rang.

"Sophie and Josh calling."

"Oh, good morning," said Mike as Sally got on the other cell. "Glad to hear from you."

"No time for chatting," said Josh. "We are calling this morning to urge you to turn on your TV. Tune into the network news immediately."

They left the breakfast table and shifted to the sofa in the living room. When the image came clear on the screen, there was the familiar image of the Stock Market and its crowd of brokers shouting and vying for attention with their bidding. The camera zoomed in to the center of the floor and immediately the dark-haired, business-suited presence of Josh and Sophie could be seen as they confronted one of the Wall Street officials.

Cutting through the background racket, Josh's voice could be heard. "We're here today as reporters to interview one of the leading interpreters of the Market crash."

"Oh, my God!" cried Sally. "Has it really happened?"

"It was bound to come," said Mike. "So this was the day."

As Mike and Sally watched, Josh and Sophie turned to the anxious official beside them.

"How do you measure this plunge compared with all the others in the past?"

"Clearly the worst."

"How will this affect investors?"

"Billions of dollars have already been lost. And I fear

we are nowhere near the end."

"Are you suggesting it may be trillions?"

"Could be."

"What will this do to the economy generally?"

"Unemployment will increase." The interviewee seemed seriously shaken. "The signs of major recession have been shadowing us in recent weeks. We're in real trouble."

"And to what do you attribute this shift in the market?"

"Very clearly the United Nations report on the virus was the driving force. The hard fact that millions have died in the epidemic has hit everyone."

As soon as the TV was shut off Mike shook his head grimly. "I'm afraid Bill has been so fascinated with his new castle that he has not been paying attention to business."

Sally's response was quick. "I think we should walk over to Ridge Road and tell him what has been happening."

"No. Not that." Mike was not about to bend. "He'd probably take big offense. The bringers of bad news are rarely welcomed. He'll find out for himself soon enough."

"I disagree," said Sally. "I've been listening to Irene. She sees her man as strangely fumbling into a new part of his life. She reports that she heard him tell his broker over the phone not to bother him with trivia. I say let's check in with her."

The move was sharply against Mike's instincts, as Sally could clearly see. But he yielded. If this was the time to serve his mate's needs, so be it. Together they crossed the street. They found Irene at the kitchen sink with the morning dishes and immediately learned that she had not heard the news.

"The Stock Market crashed?"

"The worst in history," said Sally. "Do you have any clue about Bill? Does he know?"

"Oh, I doubt it. He's been leaving his cell phone behind. You can't imagine how hard he's been pushing to get the new house moving."

"Shouldn't we tell him the news?"

Irene briefly recoiled at the idea and turned a glance toward Mike who was shaking his head in a strong negative. But as she struggled through the labyrinth of problems she turned again to Sally.

"I guess you're right. Will you come with me?"

The three walked along Hughes to Ridge Road and stepped onto the property where Bill was conferring with his contractor about a concrete driveway to the multiple garage. As soon as he saw them he turned with his eager news.

"Now we're closing in on the final entrance."

Mike accepted responsibility for being the messenger of bad tidings. "Bill, the Market took its nose dive today."

"It what?" His question had the quality of a person calling from another planet. He was not tuned to the jumbled wavelength of communication.

"Worst crash in history. We brought along your cell phone in case you want to talk to your broker."

"What the hell," he snapped, still not fully entering the historic day that followed the New Year's holiday. He grabbed the phone from Irene's hands and soon was giving orders to his Wall Street representative.

As Sally watched she felt that she was seeing an army being swallowed up by an earthquake that opened the ground beneath their feet. The hopeless anger of their friend offered no chance for a helpful hand to be extended.

When Bill finished, his face was pale and his eyes black with rage. He snapped off the phone and angrily flung the instrument far into the brush of the forest.

Sally watched sadly as Bill turned and left the site of his new castle to head back home. He didn't even bother to tell his contractor of his problem.

Together Sally and Irene and Mike followed at a distance. When Irene left them to enter her house, they bade her goodbye and stood quietly on the sidewalk in front of their own home.

"I wonder if this is the end of the world for him?" said Mike.

"This could be the saddest day, not only for Bill," was Sally's answer, "but for the whole world."

"It's something we've been watching creep closer and

closer," said Mike. "I'm beginning to wonder if even what the kids are doing with Earth Family will make any difference. You are right. This may be the beginning of the end."

Sally did a 180 degree turn-around. She shook him by the shoulders, as she often did. "Stop that! We don't need a dose of pessimism at this hour!"

"So what is the good news today? Tell me."

Sally was stalled for the moment. "I don't know." She turned toward their front door and walked up the driveway with Mike following. "I don't know," she grumbled again as she opened the door.

When they stepped into the living room a special glow of light was the first thing that caught their attention.

Sally called out her protest. "Did you leave the computer running again?"

Mike hesitated for only an instant. "I didn't turn it on at all." Sally walked toward the corner of the living room prepared to snap off the power, and then she saw on the monitor the image of the Internet. As she stood in front of the screen the picture gave way to a typed message.

"Welcome home. We've been waiting for you."

"It's Sophie here. We thought you might need some extra encouragement."

Sally called out. "Mike, it's our mentors!"

He came quickly to stand beside her. Immediately the image on the screen was supplemented with voices coming over the tiny speakers. Josh was giving voice to the printed words. "Remember, the darkest hour always comes just before the dawn."

Sally found her emotions torn to shreds. "But the horrible fact is that millions have died around the world, and this is only the beginning. There's no dawn in sight. The worst is yet to come."

"Very true," said Josh. "For you this will be a time of retreat. Your big assignment is to help your world with one call. 'Wake up!'"

By the end of February the truth for America and

Europe was deadly. Uncountable thousands had been afflicted. Sierra College closed its doors. Sally no longer commuted to Sacramento. Tad's car sales dropped to zero. He and Jeannie learned to wear dust filter masks when they had to venture out into the town.

Home became an intense focus for all four of them, with TV and Internet capturing much of their attention. Mike produced some historic facts in response to Tad's digging for more information.

"This is not the first. At the beginning of the 20th Century Asia lost ten million people to the 'plague.' In Medieval Europe bubonic plague took a quarter of the population. And then there was a thing called Justinian's plague that started in 542 A.D. and killed 100 million over a period of years."

To Sally it seemed that Tad was daily more disturbed by the development. He continued to drive hard with questions. "How many do you think have died here in Grass Valley?"

Mike shook his head. "I doubt that reports in the Union can cover the situation. The paper is now less than half its normal size. I've heard that four of their reporters have died, and the press room is cut 'way down."

Jeannie added a tragic neighborhood statistic. "The last time Alan and I walked Lidster Avenue, just our one long block, we counted five houses abandoned. Nobody living there anymore."

Sally with heavy heart shared her news. "I talked to Irene on the phone this morning. She's afraid that Little Billy may have caught the bug. Bill's in New York and she doesn't know whether to call him or not."

Mike was quick with his questions. "Will she need help to get to the hospital?"

"She phoned them. They said wait till she's sure. And, anyway, they're completely full."

"Should you maybe check in on her?" Mike offered his question with heavy caution, obviously concerned about possible contagion.

Sally slipped into silence, reaching for closer contact

with Sophie and Josh. She found encouragement. At last she smiled at Mike. “I think you may be right this time.”

“Be sure to wear your dust mask.”

The sky was loaded with heavy clouds that blocked out the noonday sun. She crossed the street quickly. Irene met her in wordless anxiety and led the way immediately to Little Billy’s bedside where Jan sat holding his hand. What Sally saw confirmed her worst fears. His breathing was noisy and harsh to the point where he could not even cry. His cheeks were drained of blood to pasty white. Eyes clamped shut.

Sally slipped her mask up to her forehead, bent close and hugged Jan with a compassion that had no limits. “How long has he been wheezing like this?”

Jan started to answer but her voice was choked with invisible tears. She coughed hard and cleared her throat and tried again. “He’s been this way since he woke up.” She rose to her feet and stared helplessly into Sally’s eyes. “Isn’t there something we can do?”

“I don’t know. There has never been a sickness like this.” She returned to the bedside. “I really think you ought to call Bill. Don’t gamble.”

Without questioning, Irene reached for the cell phone on the bureau, while Sally touched the tiny boy’s forehead with longing that she might somehow bring relief to his misery, and to his mother and grandmother as well. She understood clearly that the phone company’s loss of skilled personnel had created severe breakdowns in many locales.

Irene reported that all the lines were busy and again came to stand close to the bed. “This will be very hard on Bill. Ever since the market crashed he’s been more depressed than I’ve ever seen before. I don’t know if he can handle… “ Her words trailed off into empty silence.

Sally took the phone from her tensed up hands and called the hospital. Their answer was the same as Irene had reported. Totally full beyond capacity.

She stayed by the bedside until at last a connection was made with Bill and he swore he would be on the next plane home.

She watched Little Billy's breathing grow ever more labored. Jan's anxiety for her boy hovered close to the breaking point. In her deepest heart of hearts Sally reached again for understanding and help from Sophie and Josh. What she found was a quiet acceptance of the present real moment without any forecast of what might lie ahead. After what seemed like endless time she turned again to Irene.

"I think I should check in with my people back home. Be sure to let me know immediately of any changes."

Irene reached out both hands to grip Sally's. "Is there no end to this horror?"

"Nobody knows. The government is fumbling. The medical people are scrambling for a solution. So far as we know there has never been anything like this in the history of the planet."

Before slipping out the front door Sally repositioned her dust mask. As she crossed Lidster Avenue she was haunted by how silent it seemed. No people in their yards. No cars on the street. Only two houses poured wisps of smoke from their fireplace chimneys. What a strange world.

She climbed the front steps to their porch and was awed on entering the living room to find Mike and Tad and Jeannie sitting in a circle with Sophie and Josh. Their mentors appeared as the familiar white-haired joggers which she and Mike had met at White Cloud.

As she settled into a straight-back chair, Sophie spoke positively. "Jeannie called us on the phone because she is worried about the family and what your chances for survival may be."

Tad picked up immediately on her introductory words. "Mom, we've had a wonderful time talking with Josh and Sophie!"

Jeannie raced ahead with a confession of inner change. "My worries about survival were just the opening of a door. We've been struggling for an hour with the Big Picture."

"Your young people," Josh added, "are 'way up front when it comes to relating to the present crisis."

Sally glanced quickly at Mike and found him smiling and nodding his head.

Sophie steered the conversation swiftly toward the important issues. "Why don't you two summarize for your mother the 'big stuff' we've been talking about."

Tad and Jeannie exchanged a glance for agreement as to who should start. The brother deferred to his sister.

"I think the first thing we did was to admit that we human beings have become voracious consumers. That was the word Josh slipped in. 'Voracious' meaning endlessly hungry, gluttonous. But we don't have to stay that way. We don't have to eat up the planet Earth's resources until there's nothing left."

Sally was surprised as Mike interrupted with a confession which he offered directly to her. "I have been blaming American business for most of this, as you know all too well. I ask your forgiveness, because everybody is responsible. The poor as well as the rich. Everybody."

She reached out to touch his hand, which had been offered across the space that separated them.

"The answer," Jeannie continued, "is what Tad poured into our conversation today. He is still the philosophical leader of our Earth Family movement, even though Alan is filling in as chairman. Tell her, Tad."

"Yeah. I'll try. But first let's be clear. Earth Family is not limited to Grass Valley. All of us have been trying to keep close to Internet, plugging the story. And now there are hundreds of local groups spread across the country that are talking up the picture of what has to be done."

Sally watched her son with growing wonder. Still only in his early twenties and he had developed a vision of leadership that reached strongly into the future. His whole being seemed full of light.

"Our job is composed of four things. First we meet together in small groups to share our experience and reach for a better future. Second we get our consumer habits in leash so that we devour the least possible. Third we choose a vocation that will help us work as healers of Earth's wounds. And, finally, we spread the word. That's our Internet function."

Sally was thrilled with the simplicity of the job Tad had outlined, but the realities of the current world problem drove her to voice her doubts. "Isn't the virus epidemic going to ruin all the plans you hope to fulfill? I mean, death is stalking everywhere. Nobody is immune." She swept her gaze around the circle hoping against hope that her challenge would not be allowed to stand.

Josh spoke quietly. "Your concern is important, but the truth is that death has always been on hand to throw roadblocks in the human pathway. Today what's happening is not just the death of human bodies. A cultural death is underway. The culture that saw Earth as a thing to exploit is dying and soon will be only a historic memory." He paused and laid a hand over his heart. "The Internet is changing the world because it's also an 'inner-net'."

"Mom," cried Jeannie, "there's a new age coming!"

As she was speaking the phone rang, and Mike went to answer. Sally watched his face and was fascinated at the change of expression that swept across his cheeks and eyes and mouth as he listened.

"Yes. I'll tell her. Yes. Thank you. Thank you very much." He returned the phone to its cradle and came back to stand beside his chair, with his eyes focused on Sally. For a long moment he stalled in silence and then announced with a rare flourish.

"Well, my dear, this time you are the winner." He paused to dramatize his message with a wave of hands and a bowing of his head. "No, not a sweepstakes. Much bigger. That was Mr. Carlson on the phone. He wanted me to tell you that the Board of Directors of Venture Dress studied and restudied your video tape of their El Salvador operation —- and they have agreed to go along with your suggestions."

Sally jumped up from where she was sitting and threw her arms around her husband's body. "They did it! They did it!"

"Yes, they did," said Mike. "Your capitalist company has joined hands with the environmental movement. I never believed it would happen, but it did."

"I'm so relieved," said Sally as she turned to the circle of her most intimate fellow travelers.

Sophie came to stand close to her and Mike and spoke with joyous humor. "Once again we are finding evidence that two polar personalities, with opposing points of view, can come together as family." She waved her hands in a come-on gesture to the others, and Tad and Jeannie with Josh joined in a great collective hug.

"I only wish Sally could do the same for Bill Gordon." That was Mike conclusive word.

"I only wish," Sally echoed, "that you would stop dumping it all on me. If any help is going to come to Bill it surely will be from 'We'."

As they were all standing together in the center of the living room, the doorbell rang and Sally went to answer. It was Irene. There were tears on her cheeks. "Little Billy didn't make it."

Internet

Three days elapsed before the funeral for Bill Gordon Junior could be completed, and during that time, while Sally and Mike did their utmost to serve the family across the street, they found themselves in irritating disagreement with each other. Because the Virus M-178 epidemic showed no signs of abating, Mike threw all his weight in favor of abandoning traditional formalities and getting the casket into the earth as quickly as possible. Sally insisted that such a course would add spiritual damage to the already battered Gordons.

The visit to their friends began immediately after Bill's arrival from New York. They found him plunged into grief, with emotions far more shattered than they had ever seen before. In silence, together, they wrapped arms around him in loving comfort, which he accepted without resistance. The loss of grandson hit him a terrible blow.

Sally was glad to hold hands with Irene and Jan who were able to accept the reality of Little Billy's passing with much more calm. Andy mostly stood in the background keeping himself aloof from the family struggle.

With Bill in almost total retreat, Sally was pleased that Mike volunteered to make arrangements with the funeral establishment. What he found was a backlog of burials that would put a severe delay on their need for completion. He worked out a new plan, which he shared with the family.

"If it's all right with you, I'll get the juvenile casket and a pick-up truck and find a couple of grave diggers. I'll do it right away. You won't have to be bothered with the details."

Sally kept silence till after the program was agreed to and Mike left to work out the various parts. Then she launched into a discussion of how family and friends would travel to the cemetery, a totally different plan from what she knew Mike was envisioning.

"And I am willing to serve as coordinator and 'minister'," she declared, and found grateful acceptance from Irene, with Bill agreeing in stunned silence.

When she and Mike at last were back home and the full plan was revealed, he snapped at her with heated words.

"So you're willing to expose everybody to a lot more of the 'bug'? That's lousy! Why didn't you leave well-enough alone?"

"Because that's not what they wanted! That's not what they need!"

The trip to the cemetery proceeded smoothly with everybody wearing dust masks. The brief service that Sally supplied, while not wearing her mask, was climaxed in the lowering of the casket into the ground. Each of the family and friends dropped a symbolic clod of earth onto the top of the wooden box.

She rejoiced that a half dozen of Jan's Earth Family friends were able to join in the service. She watched with special keenness how Bill leaned heavily on Irene's arm. As they turned to leave the gravesite, Bill flashed a glance at Sally and muttered gruffly just three words.

"See you later."

Mike stayed by her side as the people slowly walked back to their cars. She continued to stand by the open hole as they waited for the return of the gravediggers. The noontime beauty of the grassy hillside, surrounded by pine trees and scattered oaks, entered into her heart and brought relief from the tension that she had been feeling. She reached out a friendly hand to her husband who seemed increasingly restless. She knew he had to wait for the return of the special diggers he had arranged for.

"We need to get out of here as soon as possible," he grumbled.

She answered with all gentleness. "Mike, it will do you a world of good to relax. Your mask is certainly okay protection. Look at the beautiful hillside." She pulled him around to take in the vista that stretched away into the forest.

When they turned back to the gravesite, there were the two grave diggers with their shovels, without masks, starting the work of filling in the hole, and they began to sing. For Sally it was not a familiar song, and also, she was sure, it was not a normal thing for such workmen to indulge in.

They came to the finale of their lyric and Sally was moved to question them. "That was a beautiful bit of music. Do you always sing at the graves you dig?"

The couple paused in their shovel work, and one of them spoke warmly. "We saw that you two were in need of new inspiration, so that's what you now have!"

Sally felt Mike grab her hand with rising excitement. "Hey, I know you! You are Josh and Sophie, aren't you?"

The couple bowed in acknowledgement, and Sally could see clearly that one of the workmen was indeed feminine.

"Isn't it about time," Sophie began, "to pour the oil of acceptance on your irritations with each other?"

Josh added more help. "The heavy burden of the world-shaking events that you are having to live with is something you two can carry together. What you have been doing lately is tossing your Mt. Everest of pain back and forth at each other. It's time to cool it."

Sally turned and found Mike staring into her eyes.

"I'm sorry, sweetheart," he whispered.

She reached up and kissed him.

Sophie carried the dialogue forward into new territory. "You two have been plunged into the toughest kind of problems that people ever have to face. Death is pressing in upon you from every side. And you haven't yet learned how to handle it."

Sally leaned hard against Mike's body and let her feeling flow out. "I tried to comfort the Gordons in their loss of Little Billy, but in the midst of the stuff I was reading during the funeral service, I realized I didn't know what I was talking about. Tell us, please, what is the meaning of death?"

The two mentors jabbed their shovels into the pile of earth still waiting to be pushed onto the casket and walked around the open hole to be closer. Josh spoke simply.

"The best place to begin is to say that death is a mystery. Your rational left-brained minds are not designed to deal with it. What you see one moment is a body full of life and the next moment empty. What you do not see is that the consciousness that formed the body has now laid it aside and is going on to create new life forms."

"Wait a minute," cried Mike. "Are you telling us that consciousness does not die?"

"Of course. Your habit of thinking that consciousness is only a product of your physical brain is exactly backwards. Think carefully. Consciousness forms bodies. The function of bodies is to inform consciousness."

Sally reached out with excitement. "What you are saying then is that the hopes and dreams of humankind through all the ages, that there is life beyond death, really is true?"

Sophie interrupted. "We feel that is enough new thinking to keep you busy for a while. We are going to get back to work with our shovels."

"One more thing," Josh offered. "You have been in the habit of calling on us for help when you have special needs. We want you to think carefully about how you can keep in touch with us constantly—-twenty-four hours a day."

Sally felt her forehead skin wrinkle up as it always did when puzzles without solutions confronted her. She turned to Mike and found a fellow traveler.

Their mentors made short work of the grave filling, waved goodby and vanished across the grassy hillslope. Sally and Mike with wonder filling their souls walked back to the borrowed pickup truck and headed for home.

The hard winter of the year 2020 A.D. gave way to summer without any signs of the Virus M-178 epidemic slacking off. U.N. statistics continued to push the totals toward a billion lives lost. The global economy sank deeper into confusion with multi-national corporations in major retreat. Airline travel shrank steadily and many companies were driven into bankruptcy and closure.

But there were exceptions. Sally pursued her work to create dress designs for Venture and to pressure Mr. Carlson for reports on their El Salvador work. She rejoiced that the company's willingness to put persons ahead of profits was paying dividends. One of their major programs was protecting and building the health of the workers. The number of deaths in the little El Salvador community had dropped steadily.

Close to home there were other exceptions. In the Grass Valley-Nevada City area the most hopeful movement of all was being promoted by the Earth Family young people. Mike served as advisor and Alan and Tad shared leadership roles. Day after day they pushed the "Four-point Program" to help neighbors, and the community as a whole, to take responsibility for healing the environment.

Sally rejoiced to watch members of the group snap on their dust masks and go door to door encouraging householders to start backyard vegetable gardens, and to offer practical help. She and Mike were especially fascinated to see that several families had even plowed up their front lawns to add growing space. The message the young people delivered was very strong.

"We're not coming to the end of the world. It's up to all of us working together to change the way we live on planet Earth—-from exploiters to a loving family."

That was also the Earth Family agenda when the group met weekly in Tad and Jeannie's living room. Sally and Mike were careful to stay in the background to avoid any appearance of interfering.

On one especially hot Sunday afternoon late in July Alan called to order the more than twenty committee members who filled all the seating and all the carpet space available. So many of them chose to push their masks up into a forehead position that Sally decided it was a new dress code.

"Okay," said Alan, "we have a big agenda today. I'd like to start with a very personal announcement." He stood up and took a couple of steps toward where Jeannie was sitting. "We have decided that it is time for us to get married and start a new family."

The applause was wild as he bent down and shared a kiss with her. Sally watched the faces of other couples who were sitting close together, and a lively intuition swept into her consciousness. The decision of Jeannie and her man, in the face of the tragic world scene, would probably give encouragement for several more to follow suit.

Alan moved promptly into the business of the day. "First let's have reports of your neighborhood contacts, beginning with Nevada City groups."

The message was mixed. Some gardens were flourishing. Others, complete failure. Frequent local meetings were bringing families into close relationships. They were finding mutual helpfulness. One of the girls that Sally had not met before spoke a message that started tears in her eyes.

"My father died from the virus, and also my younger brother. But our neighborhood group has filled in the empty space for mother and me. Every day somebody comes over and gives a loving word or hand. I'm sure mother would have fallen apart without this support. She is even reaching out herself to help another family across the street who lost. . . " Her voice trailed off into choked silence and Sally guessed that the girl had lost someone else too close to talk about.

When the reporting was completed Alan turned to Tad. "What's the current story about our Internet connections?"

Tad waved his arms in a sweeping gesture to include everyone present. "I'm amazed at how fast this has grown. Everyday we're talking to people all over the place: all along the Pacific Coast from San Diego to Seattle and even beyond. Which one of you is it who knows Spanish and is talking to Mexico City?"

One of the boys waved his hand to confirm.

Tad swept on. "And our message is racing across more frontiers everyday: Chicago, Denver, Little Rock, Canada. What I'm beginning to see is that we could be even more effective if we had a common meeting place where we could set up our monitors and keep closer to each other."

Sally was heartened by the energizing dream her son was projecting. One of the boys reached for clearness.

"Do you mean like your garage—-like where we built the globe for the County Fair?"

"Not there. Not nearly big enough. I'm thinking about a place for 20 tables, and more. A place where we can really get it all together."

Sally glanced sideways at Mike and whispered, "Did you know about this idea?"

He shook his head. "He's been imagining stuff faster than I can keep up with him."

Tad tossed a question out to the group. "Does anyone know of any facility?"

A girl from the opposite end of Lidster Avenue spoke up. "The house next to us has been empty for many months. Would that work?"

Tad meditated for a moment and then observed. "It wouldn't be different from what we have right here. I don't think spreading our work around in half a dozen little rooms would do it."

Sally smiled to herself. *Statesman Tad knows what he really wants.* And then the familiar voice of Jan sounded from near the door to the kitchen.

"I can't speak for the Gordon family, but we have a new house over on Ridge Road that isn't finished yet. It's huge."

Tad was quick to confirm. "We've all seen the 'Castle.' But your dad isn't about to let a bunch like us butt into his dream. Is he?"

"I don't know the answer. The reason I brought up the subject is that I've been watching my father. Week after week he seems more depressed. He hasn't gone near the house since the Stock Market crash." She fell into a moment of silence. "The idea came to me as we were talking about Earth Family needs, that we might volunteer to do the finishing work for him in exchange for permission to set up our Internet shop."

A sudden stir of excitement swept through the gathering. Several voices were raised almost at once.

"Hey! It's a great idea!"

"We have a lot of finishing skills right here."

"I could do some of the painting."

"Hold it," cried Tad. "The big hurdle is getting Mr. Gordon to say, 'Go ahead.' How about it Jan? Are you the one to make the case for us?"

Sally watched as Jan shook her head. "He won't listen to me. He never does."

And then Mike's voice entered the arena of discussion. "I think you should form a committee of three or four and visit him with your proposition. Go to him openly as Earth Family. I think he may surprise you."

The business of forming a committee and talking through the various ways to present their case took much of the remaining time before adjournment. When Sally at last was alone with Mike she found her curiosity about her husband's last word too important to ignore.

"You think Bill will surprise them? Why? Do you have some inside information that I have missed?"

Mike smiled with a conspiratorial grin. "You apparently have forgotten an important event."

"Don't play games. I don't know what you are talking about."

"Let me put it this way. If a person is haunted by guilt feelings because of some stupid act he did in the distant past, isn't he likely to grab at a chance to make amends?"

Swiftly the light dawned for Sally. "Oh! I see what you mean. Like the smashing of the Fairgrounds globe?"

"Why not?"

It was not until the middle of the following week that Tad was able to share the outcome of their appointment with Mr. Gordon.

"We sat down with Bill and Irene. Jan and Andy were there too. The first thing we learned was some really bad news. It was Irene who told us. Their doctor has found that Bill has colon cancer. He's going in for surgery on Monday."

Sally caught Mike's eyes and they shared silently the tragic memory of their friend's path through life. Tad continued.

"Alan was very good in his presentation. And each of us pitched in to make the case for how we could help with the finishing work. I was very impressed with how grim Mr. Gordon was through all our sharing. He really is depressed. I don't think he cared at all. But in the end —-you won't believe it! —-he said he would go along with us if we will pick up where he left off."

Sally wanted to be very clear about the "agreement," that it really included more than just the finishing work. "Did Bill really say you can use the 'Castle' as headquarters for the Earth Family and your Internet work?"

"For sure! That's what it was all about."

Mike shook his head in silence and Sally knew that his doubts still had deep roots.

By Saturday the 'committee in charge' had mobilized Earth Family workers and all sorts of tools and supplies, and at 8 a.m. the masked company converged on the Ridge Road castle. Sally insisted that Mike attend with her the "opening ceremony" in spite of his "I'll believe it when I see it" stance.

Jan brought the keys and did what amounted to a formal unlocking. As the group walked through the interior to make a first time survey it was clear that vandals had left their mark. A broken window on the back side provided access. On the marble walls of the big living room graffiti had been scrawled: WELCOME TO HELL.

Tad called out for everyone to hear. "We've come to transform this place into exactly the opposite. Who wants to volunteer to scrub that off?"

Swiftly a dozen different jobs got underway and Sally, after Mike had nudged her, told Alan that they had other responsibilities to attend to.

As they left the beautifully forested property and began their walk back toward Lidster Avenue she mumbled a message through her dust mask. "You don't have to be so negative. Give them a chance to see what they can do."

Mike's response was equally muffled. "I'm not worried about the kids. It's Bill Gordon who is the unknown. He can still screw up the whole thing, even if he's going to be out of circulation with cancer surgery."

During Sunday afternoon the work crew continued at their tasks, and when Tad and Jeannie returned home after sunset they had a fascinating report to make.

"My future husband surprised us all," said Jeannie with spirit that covered her weariness. "He told us that, if we all agree, we can have a live-in caretaker at the Castle."

"Well, that makes big sense," said Mike. "Help to stop any future vandals."

"But who would take on a job like that?" Sally asked.

"It's a couple who were helping Alan's next door elderly neighbors. The old folks are moving to New York, and the helping-couple need a new place to move to."

Mike pushed hard. "So who's going to pay for their service? Earth Family doesn't have that kind of money."

Tad added to the report in a tone of voice that sounded almost apologetic. "Alan said they said they don't need any wages."

Sally's curiosity climbed higher. "So who are these people?"

"He said they are Mr. and Mrs. Delbert Mundo who originally came from South Africa. I think maybe they are native Africans. But anyway, the group agreed 100 percent that it would be a good idea to have live-in caretakers."

When she and Mike were alone at bedtime, Sally laid a gentle hand on her husband's arm. "I'm suspicious about those new people that Alan contacted. No wages? Doesn't that stir your curiosity?"

"Why don't you ask our mentors for the inside dope?"

"That's exactly what I am hinting at. Let's."

She reached for her cell phone and immediately made contact.

"Good evening," came the familiar voice of Sophie. "We've been waiting."

Sally plunged immediately with her hunch. "Are you

acquainted with the Delbert Mundos?"

Josh answered. "Call me Del, if you like."

"I knew it!" said Sally as she turned to Mike with the news. "It had to be! Our mentors are also taking up with the next generation!"

But when she spoke again into the phone it was silent.

She returned to Mike with rising excitement. "I wonder, could this be the great breakthrough? Everybody in contact!"

His response was like brakes on a runaway car. "What about us? We still haven't learned how to obey. They want us to listen to them 24 hours a day. Remember? We still are off-again, on-again."

Sally's shame was like a child's, being caught in the midst of a no-no. "But we don't know how to do it." After a moment of silence she whispered, "All right. Let's try again."

In the morning when she wakened she found Mike sitting up with his pillow cushioning the headboard of their bed. He seemed to be in a deeply meditative mood. As she turned over to face him he spoke softly.

"I had a dream. About Josh and Sophie. They were standing on top of a hill, beckoning us to climb. That's a first for me."

Swiftly Sally sat up beside him. "Mike! I too dreamed! You and I were in a sailboat. Sophie and Josh were blowing the wind in the sails."

Mike chuckled. "Maybe that's the breakthrough you were reaching for. Twenty-four hours a day includes our dream world. And every other hour too. That's very hard."

On the day after Bill Gordon's surgery, Sally and Mike paid him a visit at the hospital. They found him clinging hard to Irene's hand as she sat next to the bed. They pulled off their dust masks.

"We're happy to see you survived," Mike began cheerily. Grim silence was the patient's only answer with eyes that stared blankly at the ceiling of the room.

Sally was not surprised for she had watched his downward slide of spirit for more weeks than she wanted to count.

"He's very tired," was Irene's brief response, and she nodded lovingly at the visitors.

Sally moved closer with her natural next question. "So what's the doctor's report?"

Irene shook her head silently with a frown that said very clearly, "Not good."

Mike's response was to step close to the bed and take Bill's free hand in his. "Hey, pal, we're with you all the way."

Sally's pulse beat strong with admiration for her husband's loving care. He was a "best friend" who never wavered in giving his support, even though he disagreed totally with the values Bill had pursued so unrelentingly.

Bill turned his head to stare at the face that was hovering over him. "What the hell! Nobody's going anywhere—-not with the damned virus on the loose. When I get out of this trap I should go out into the open air, without my mask, and breathe in all the air my lungs can hold!"

Sally was stunned by his tragic outburst. She stepped close, to add her hand to Irene's grip, and she found herself moved to use language she never dreamed would ever cross her lips.

"Bill Gordon, stop that nonsense! The world is not coming to an end and neither are you! Look how many people there are who love you! Irene! Me! Mike! And your kids! And all the Earth Family! And many more! We want you to promise you will wear your mask, always, when out in the open." She paused, out of breath, and wondered, *Am I off the track?*

He stared up at her for an instant and then closed his eyes. She couldn't tell whether he was surrendering to her demand or shutting it out.

Irene signaled with a shake of her head that this would have to be the end for their conversation. Time to break off. Sally was glad that Irene chose to follow them into the hallway; her spirit had grown and matured so swiftly in recent months. Her simple words struck home.

"Bill is falling apart. First it was the Market Crash, then Little Billy's death, and now the doctor says that in three or four months we should know whether the cancer comes back or not. I just pray he'll make it somehow."

Mike delivered a gentle pat on her back. "Irene, without your constant loving care Bill would have caved in a long time ago. I'm proud of you."

On the way home in the Honda Sally pulled the cell phone from Mike's belt and announced that she wanted to call their mentors.

"I'm sure they'll be waiting for us," Mike declared.

"I feel we're at a dead end." She punched in the numbers and immediately the familiar loving voices were on the line with Josh speaking first.

"Where are you now?"

Sally puzzled for an instant. "Why, we're driving west on East Main Street."

"No, no! Where are you in your spirits?"

"Oh. Sorry. —-Ah, —-I was just saying to Mike that I felt we were at a dead end with Bill Gordon."

Sophie spoke up. "Do you remember the principle we gave you the last time we were together?"

Sally felt her confusion growing. "The principle? I guess we should have written it on one of the calling cards." She turned to her husband. "Mike, did you write it down?"

Sophie interrupted. "Already we have made it clear that you don't need any more calling cards."

Sally repeated for Mike's benefit. "Don't need cards."

Josh followed through with words that she felt as reprimand. "You cannot hope to help Bill unless you heed the final, ultimate word that we gave you. Try to remember. When we were all together at Little Billy's gravesite, what did we say to you? What was the last thing we said?"

Sally found tears welling up from her heart, which was torn with longing for the healing of the Gordon family, who for her had come to represent the agony of the whole of planet Earth.

"Now I remember! You told us that we needed to keep in touch with you 24 hours a day. That was it, wasn't it?" Again the awful words of confession came pouring out. "But we don't know how to do that."

Mike whispered to her as he turned the corner onto Lidster. "We goofed again, didn't we? Tell them, from now on, we will really work at this!

Sally repeated his message and the phone went silent. She felt the Honda slow down to a crawl, and then Mike spoke, and his humble message struck deep.

"I think what they want us to do, in our heart of hearts, is to listen for their guidance. We don't have to see them in person to do that. We don't have to get on the phone to talk to them. We just have to go inside, and they will be there."

"Thank you, darling," was Sally's humble response, and then they were home.

Mike swung the car into their driveway. To her joy and delight, there on the front porch, she saw Sophie and Josh waiting for them, once again fulfilling the promise that they would always be present.

Beyond White Cloud

The "24 Hours a Day" principle proved harder than Sally and Mike imagined as they struggled to keep faithful. Sally worked at remembering while she prepared meals, while she listened to Tad and Jeannie report their progress, while she talked on the phone with Mr. Carlson. But frequently she was distracted and lost the joy of their mentor's presence. Her best time had become bedtime as she reviewed the day and practiced letting go and letting Sophie and Josh take her into sleep.

Mike shared with her his own growth in classes that had begun again. He exulted that during lectures, more than ever in the past, he was finding new and very powerful words coming from deep within to inspire his students.

July gave way to August and Sally and Mike rejoiced in the daily reports their young people brought back from the Castle.

"We're up and running," said Tad at last, "and the results are pouring in. Internet is red hot! The story is getting told world-wide!"

Jeannie's word was sweetly intimate. "You really would love the way the Del Mundos are taking care of the place—- and taking care of us. They're even fixing lunches. Everybody adores them. They've become the Mom and Pop of the Earth Family."

"But there's a really terrific thing happening," Tad exulted. "Our neighborhood groups are finding the Castle is a perfect meeting place. They're taking turns with the big hall."

Jeannie continued about the Mundo couple. "Have you seen the new car they've acquired? It's a hydrogen Honda, bright red. I love the way they drive in and out, doing shopping and errands for us all the time."

Mike intervened with a question. "Were they one of

your customers, Tad?"

"Nope. I don't know where they got it."

On the last day of September Sally met her two young people at the door as they arrived home in the evening. She found three of the Earth Family friends in their company: Jan, Andy, and Alan. The expressions in the eyes of each one as they peeked above their masks told her immediately that something was in the wind.

"Is the fire up on Highway 20 coming this way?" she demanded. That was foremost on everyone's mind. For a week the flames that began in the upper reaches of the South Yuba canyon had been covering Grass Valley and Nevada City with heavy smoke.

The young people pushed past her into the living room to where Mike was beginning to set the table for supper. Their masks came off and Alan with his customary flourish answered for the group.

"We're not here about the fire. It's under control at last. We have something else. We thought you ought to hear it early, before the word gets around."

Sally stepped close to Mike, stirred by the unusual mood that radiated from the group.

"I think I should let Jan tell the news," said Alan.

She began hesitantly. "You know how sick my dad has been. Yesterday he and my mom got the news from his surgeon that the cancer was recurring—-severely."

"Oh, how terrible," said Sally. "That's what we were afraid of."

Jan continued. "I saw in his face that the news was crushing him, but only for a minute. Then he pulled out of his shock and spoke very quietly. He said, 'I've got to rewrite my will. I've got to give my Castle to my children so they can hold it for the group they're calling the Earth Family.'"

Jan paused for a moment and then added what sounded to Sally like a footnote. "He said, 'to my children.' Not to me and Andy. He didn't even look at us when he said he would rewrite his will."

"What a strange spin," said Sally. "But all of this sounds as though his suffering has some how changed his way of thinking."

"Maybe," said Mike, forever the skeptic. Sally noted that he didn't add, "I'll believe it when I see it."

"Anyway," Alan continued, "it means that we're not using the Castle only as a temporary place. It's for keeps." And Jan and Andy nodded their heads vigorously.

On the second Saturday of October, after the family had finished breakfast and Tad and Jeannie headed for the Castle, Sally was cheered as Mike gently reached for her hand.

"Can we follow through on our trip to Sacramento?"

To her the best part of his question was the style of his touch. Their joint effort to keep close to their mentors, without ceasing, meant that both husband and wife in this marriage would reach for the "higher consciousness" as they worked through the challenges of each day.

"So you really feel that an interview with Mr. Carlson will help bring the Big Picture into sharper focus?" she asked.

"My students need to hear about the environmental breakthroughs that business can produce when they put people first. Venture Dresses has a good record, and I need to talk with him."

"Do you want me to phone and make an appointment?"

"Thanks."

As Sally headed for the phone she reached for the inner contact with Sophie and Josh that would confirm their mutual decision. In just a few moments that pathway was opened, and she and Mike climbed into the Honda with their dust masks in place. The sky was heavy with clouds, and it was cold.

As Mike backed out of the driveway he paused, for there was Jan standing anxiously at the edge of the street. Sally opened her window and leaned out.

"Are you all right, Jan? Is there trouble?"

Jan stepped close to the car. "I'm worried about Mom

and Dad. They just drove off in the Cadillac. I'm afraid for their safety."

"Do you know where they're going?"

"My dad wouldn't tell."

"I wish there were something we could do to help, but we're on the way to Sac."

Jan was appreciative of their concern and encouraged them to go on their way.

Mike headed over to Hughes Road and turned down the steep hill to East Main, which he followed until he was able to get on the freeway. No sooner did their wheels roll beyond the on-ramp than the cell phone rang.

Sally responded. "Yes? Oh, Sophie! Glad to hear from you. What's that?" Her eyes sought out Mike's in anguish. Then she said, "Would you repeat what you just said for Mike to hear?" She handed him the phone.

"Hello, Mike." It was Sophie again, and Sally could hear the muffled voice. "We are making a simple urgent request. Josh and I want you to go up to White Cloud, right away."

The phone went dead. In grim wonderment he handed it back to Sally and without further questioning took the off-ramp at Empire Street, crossed over the freeway and headed back in the direction from which they had just come.

"Something important?" he wondered with a grumble. "All right. So we're headed for the hills instead of the valley."

"What are we going to do about Mr.Carlson?" Sally mumbled through her dust mask.

"Call him. Tell him to cancel."

Sally's mood changed. "No. That's too feverish. May I remind you, with all our problems and with all our disagreements, there is one thing we agree on? When Sophie and Josh call we respond!"

Mike fell into silence, drove doggedly on the freeway past Nevada City and then along Highway 20 that led up to Washington Ridge.

At last he muttered, "Maybe there's some trouble we

don't know about."

Sally reached out with her left hand and gently laid it on his thigh in a loving affirmation of support. She watched, and his mood began to return toward more peacefulness.

As she sat quietly meditating on the strangeness of their interrupted trip to Sacramento, her thoughts slipped into rejoicing over this strip of highway they had come to love. The trees of the forest were twenty years older than when they made their first trip, taller and with sturdier trunks. The land was successfully rebuilding the ecosystem that had been stripped bare by earlier generations of humans.

A deep restfulness came over her whole body and her inmost thoughts. She spoke simply to Mike. "I'm beginning to feel that Sophie and Josh maybe are sending us back to White Cloud for something that we have not imagined before."

Mike turned his eyes briefly to look into hers and then opened the door to his own private thoughts. "I can go with that. They are the ones who have helped you and me to do more agreeing and less quarreling. If it's White Cloud we're headed for it will surely be for something important."

At last they passed Five Mile House. Suddenly the scene changed. The huge fire of July had swept along the ridge to within a mile of the restaurant and store. Stark, blackened trees with their crowns destroyed, crowded both sides of the highway. Sally mourned the shattered landscape.

Memory took her back to the beauty of this bit of Mother Earth which surrounded them on their earlier trip to White Cloud. And then a coincidence made her smile. She added an amused comment for her mate's meditation.

"We're doubling up today."

"Yeah. Not only a repeat of 20 years ago. This is also our 25th wedding anniversary."

"What a way to celebrate," Sally chuckled.

A few miles later the familiar road sign appeared, and Mike turned into the entrance to what remained of the

White Cloud picnic grounds. Sally sharpened her gaze, half expecting to see the pair of joggers, as they had in the beginning. But they were not present. *So what are we here for*? she wondered.

The fire had devastated the picnic facilities, burned tables and restrooms, left the grounds in chaos. Only tall dark ponderosas remained, without their green crowns.

As Mike drove slowly toward the site of their first encounter Sally cried out with amazement. "Look! There's the Gordons' Cadillac!"

"So that's what this is all about!" said Mike.

Beyond the luxury car they could see Bill and Irene standing face to face, in almost the same place where they themselves had stood, to the left of a surviving picnic table. Their arrival interrupted whatever exchange had been taking place. The Gordons turned to face them. Sally and Mike left the car and came to stand at a cautious distance from their friends. She noticed, lying on the ground, a pair of dust masks.

"What the hell are you doing here?" Bill cried with savage anger. "You think spying will make any difference?"

Oh no, thought Sally, *they're in the midst of a showdown of some kind.*

Mike spoke gently. "No, Bill, we're not spying. We're concerned about you and your cancer problem."

"Well, it's too late," he snapped. "This is the end of the road. The cancer's hopeless."

Irene caught Sally's eye and shook her head in silent warning. Plainly she was terrified about something. But then she spoke out. "I do not agree."

Immediately Bill cut in. "Keep quiet!"

"No, Bill. You let me speak." She turned toward Sally. "Whether he likes it or not, I will tell you. He's planning for suicide."

"She's exactly correct," Bill moaned, "I am," and he reached inside his unbuttoned jacket and out of his belt line pulled the revolver that he had brandished the day Irene escaped to the DVC. "And I'm taking her with me!"

As Sally watched, Bill automatically pointed his hand

toward them with the gun. Sally recoiled inwardly with growing shock. It became the focus of his message, which he poured out violently.

"Time has run out! I've nothing to live for! Nobody does! The end of the world is coming fast! All I want is for Irene to be with me. Whatever comes afterwards..."

His words spoke loudly to Sally that the unknown, which lay beyond death, was really a haunting puzzle for him. The black deadened trees and the broken charred bushes that surrounded them everywhere were a language that agreed with everything he was saying.

Mike interceded. "But you don't have to add murder to your plan for suicide. Irene should make her own choice."

Bill's face flushed, and he swung the gun to point directly at Irene. His words came out with confused passion. "Hell! I'm doing her a favor to take her with me! Waiting around while Earth falls apart will be nothing but terror."

As Sally watched Bill's turmoil she sensed that a new idea must be taking shape in his consciousness.

"Yeah. I'm doing her a favor. And I should do you the same favor. You two have been my best friends. All four of us should go together. The world is hopelessly lost, and you know it."

Sally found her mind flashing back through the 20 years of friendship they had shared and sensed that what he was spelling out to them now was nothing new.

Bill swung back to point the gun in their direction and Sally realized that Bill's finger on the trigger could very easily be pulled during a burst of emotion, which might come at any instant. Quietly within she spoke to herself. *If this is the time for our death, so be it.* But Mike spoke lovingly.

"Bill, you are truly kind and thoughtful to care for us as you have said. But there is one thing in your planning that I have to raise into doubt." Mike was being as conciliatory as he could possibly be. "Now I'm speaking as 'Professor of the Environment.' The end of the world is not a sure thing, yet. There are some signs of hope. Or maybe I would say it better this way. There are many groups of people who are changing their lifestyles because they are learning to love Mother Earth."

As she watched, Mike then did an act of symbolic daring. He took off his dust mask and threw it on the ground next to the other two masks. Quickly Sally followed his example.

She felt a growing need to give extra support to Irene and at last she moved. She wanted to match the symbolism of her husband's gesture. Inwardly she knew she needed to close the distance; somehow to stand beside her friend; to declare her solidarity. She took one step.

Bill shouted, "Stay where you are!" He pointed the gun directly at Sally. She retreated. *Okay, so he's determined.*

Mike launched a new approach. "Bill, why did you come up to White Cloud? You could carry out your plan just as well back in the house on Lidster."

"No way," Bill grumbled. "I wasn't about to mess up the house that Jan and Andy are going to inherit."

For Sally this felt like a strange ray of hope flashing light into the core of Bill's dark world. He was thinking positively about somebody else. His children, though remote, were still important to him.

Mike reached again. "That's great, Bill. Also, we understand, you have rewritten your will to make Jan and Andy the owners of the Castle for the benefit of the Earth Family."

Mike's words apparently unnerved his friend. As Sally watched she guessed that Bill actually had not gotten around to fixing his will at all. Mike pushed harder.

"Bill, you have such a wonderful dream. What's the block?"

Bill shook his head violently. "Don't talk to me about blocks! I don't want to see another. Ever!"

"But, Bill, blocks are the stuff that dream castles are made of. You've got lots of them over there on Ridge Road. Blocks of marble. Blocks of wood."

"Shut up! You don't know what you're talking about! There's nothing but pain over there anymore."

"Pain? What do you mean, Bill? Is there some kind of buried pain that's leaking out of your memories? Pain about blocks? Why, Bill, why?"

Sally watched with awe at her husband's reaching into the depths, with the instincts of a counselor.

"Blocks? Yeah. That's right." As Bill began groping into his buried world of memories, his revolver hand dropped to his side.

Sally reached deep into her soul. *Oh, Sophie, Josh, help us! Help us to help Bill get free!*

"Blocks. That's what did it. My father did it."

"Your father?" Mike prompted him out of his silence.

"Yeah." For an instant he seemed to drift off into another world. "When I was a five-year-old I loved to build with blocks. I wanted to build the biggest most beautiful castle in the world. But my father always knocked it down, unfinished. 'Can't have this in the middle of the floor,' he said, again and again."

As Sally stared at the Gordons, suddenly she saw standing directly behind them the shadowy figures of Sophie and Josh. At first they seemed as tall as the trees, but quickly they became regular size, dressed in jogging costumes with woolly caps protecting their white hair. She flashed a look toward Mike and he nodded back his agreement as to what they were seeing.

She spoke directly to Bill to give extra support. "We all of us have a lot of unfinished business from our childhood. I remember how my Dad said I'd never succeed at anything, because I didn't care about details."

Mike put in a cheerful observation. "Now that's all she does! Details! She's meticulous to a fault."

Irene joined the circle of support. "When it comes to money Bill is the most meticulous man in the world. I can't get near him on money. Lots of times I wished I could help him with our household accounting. But he does it all."

Bill switched his attention back and forth among the ones who were speaking their hearts. "You have reminded me of something else," he declared, with a growing sense of awe that showed in his eyes. "When I was a sophomore in high school I wanted to go out for football. My father was against it. Insisted it was too easy to get severe injury. But I was a teenager. I signed up anyway. I got along fine in practice. But when a game came along I found I was always stuck on the bench. I spoke to the coach. He always said the same thing. 'I'll send you in at the right moment.' But that moment never came. I quit. I didn't learn the truth until Irene and I got together. Her dad knew my father, and he found out that it was big money from my father to the coach that kept me out of the game."

Irene added her footnote. "When I told him about the bribery he got angry at me. Real angry!"

"The point is," Bill growled, "my father made me think I was an all-out failure. So I set out to prove him wrong. Wrong! Wrong! Wrong!"

"Bill!" cried Sally. "There could be another point to your story! Maybe your father wanted to keep you from getting hurt because he loved you!"

Bill stared at her with no sign of understanding.

Mike took hold again, and Sally sensed with rising gratitude their mentors were giving him the right words at this time of need.

"Bill, I'm glad you told us. I remember how you and I walked up to Sierra College, side by side, to start our careers. We both climbed to the top. I as professor, you as the best brain on Wall Street. Now here we are, you and I, right on the threshold of our biggest assignment ever. For both of us the challenge is the same. Together you and I can work for the breakthrough that will save Mother Earth."

Bill stared, uncomprehending. "What are you talking about?"

Sally picked up the thread. "I wish we could show you everything your two kids are doing for the repair of the earth environment. They are absolutely astounding. In fact their whole generation is the most wonderful thing that has happened to our world."

Sally pulled out all the stops. She knew that she was

doubtless exaggerating, but, after all, the hour called for bold actions beyond the highest reaches of imagination, and best of all she saw Sophie and Josh move silently to stand very close to their confused neighbor.

"Bill, you have been cut off from what's been happening in the last couple of years. Let us bring you up to date. Our kids, yours and ours, have created a movement that is pulling Joe and Mary Citizen right into the middle of action to save the planet. Thousands of people are seriously at work changing their American lifestyle toward sustainability."

Bill shook his head in disbelief. "They're doing what?"

"I'm not surprised that you haven't heard. Your cancer has grabbed your attention. But now hear this. Jan and Andy and Tad and Jeannie are right now standing on the most important threshold of the movement. They have completed the finishing work on the Castle and are now working hard to spread the message to the whole country, and beyond."

Irene burst into the picture. "Bill, wouldn't it be wonderful if the kids could really make the Castle the center for saving planet Earth?"

Sally saw that Bill seemed confused at first, but as he groped his way into the vision being laid out, his face brightened up for the first time. "You're saying that maybe there's something we can do to help?"

"For sure," said Mike. "There's a chance for a real breakthrough. But it's going to take a lot of money."

A break in the clouds overhead let a shaft of sunlight brighten the campground as Sally gave Bill more and more details. "The kids are dreaming big business. Radio station. Television. Internet. Publishing headquarters. You name it, they're ready to go to work on it."

Bill turned to Irene. "Really? Do you think we could help out?"

"With you, Bill, I'm ready." She stretched her arms up toward the sky where the blue was showing at last. Sally felt a thrill of hope. Irene's strength could be counted on to move them into a new life.

Mike nodded to Sally with a note of caution. Then he turned to the Gordons. He stepped forward a couple of paces, close to Bill and held out his hand. “How about letting me take charge of the gun? Okay?”

Bill looked down absentmindedly at the revolver and easily passed it into Mike’s hand, hardly noticing while his friend moved the bullets into a waiting pocket. Bill had another comment to make.

“My cancer problem may get in the way. I’m afraid it can stop me before we can fix all that needs to be fixed.”

Sally stepped close to her husband and together they wrapped arms around Bill in a deep love-filled embrace. As she looked over his shoulder her eyes followed the movement that Sophie and Josh were now making. They left their position behind the Gordons and stood one on each side of the picnic table. It had been scorched by the big fire, but had survived and was sturdy.

Sally caught the silent message from their mentors and spoke directly to Bill. “I think it’s time for us to step out onto a new frontier. Medicine has not been able to help you, but there are other methods of healing. If you’re willing, Bill, we should try to make contact with our Higher Power.”

“Oh, yes!” cried Irene. “That’s what we need! I’ve been wishing for a long time for some new way to help.”

Bill glanced back and forth to search the faces that surrounded him. Sally was totally sure that all he saw was love. He spoke humbly and with a growing sense of awe filling his face. “All right. Can’t win without trying.”

Mike and Sally helped him stretch out on his back on the waiting picnic table. The mentors added their hands to those of the three family people. Five pairs of hands gently touched Bill from his head and shoulders to his abdomen.

A powerful silence descended upon them. Sally wondered whether Bill could feel the hands of Sophie and Josh. This was so different from anything she had ever dreamed of.

Bill had been involved in marital violence and questionable business practices, and was probably guilty of illegal manipulation of the Stock Market. She turned all of these stumbling blocks over to their mentors and directed her spirit inward with loving concern for their battered friend. She sang silent joy for the presence of Sophie and Josh. And for her beloved husband. And for Irene.

The time sped by, again feeling like hours, but the reality could be counted as minutes. Bill sucked in a deep breath of air and opened his eyes. He caught a vision of Irene's beaming face and opened his arms to her. She bent over in a shared embrace that brought tears close to Sally's eyes, for she heard the penitential words he whispered into his wife's ears.

"Please forgive me for all the harshness I dumped on you all the years past."

As Irene planted a kiss on his waiting lips, Sally remembered that they were in fact not legally married. Mike moved in close to Sally's side and helped Bill to sit upright on the table top. Here truly was a new dimension of family. From the closeness of the two couples a new sound of joy spread out through the forest. Bill was reaching for the reality of family. He swung around to Irene and spoke humbly for everyone to hear.

"Irene, will you marry me?"

She joined him on the table top with an embrace that told Sally she was ready. This was a huge part of his healing.

"This time we're going to do it right," he declared, beaming his word to Sally and Mike. "With your help we'll have the wedding we skipped 30 years ago."

Sally held back the words she was tempted to share, because they belonged solely to her experience with Mike. *Now at last we have escaped the marry-go-round forever.* Instead she spoke of her favorite truth.

"Mike and I discovered 20 years ago that the purpose of marriage is to create family. I think you two have made a marvelous new beginning."

Bill slid off the table top to stand squarely on his two feet. "I think Irene and I should go back home and get to work on our new dream, since I don't really know how much time I have. I'll depend on you two to connect me with the young people as I finally rewrite my will."

"We'll be available all the way," said Mike.

"And that will be only the beginning." Bill took Irene by the hand and headed for the Cadillac, and Sally turned and found herself face to face with their mentors.

Josh spoke warmly. "Congratulations. As of today you two have fulfilled your promotion."

"Promotion?" Mike spoke with joyful curiosity.

"Exactly," said Sophie and pointed to the Cadillac as Bill was climbing in. "You loved them into a new world. So now we can say farewell to you. You have reached full stature."

She reached for Josh's hand and they turned to walk toward the Gordon's car for some unannounced purpose.

With Mike at her side Sally listened as Bill started the engine, and then she and Mike grabbed each other's hand with awed excitement, for their mentors were climbing into the back seat of the Cadillac. The car turned around and headed for Highway 20.

Mike and Sally faced each other with love filling their hearts.

"Hello, Josh," said Sally. And Mike responded with joyful laughter, "Hello, Sophie."